Zombies of the Science Fair

DON'T MISS THE REST OF THE
SIXTH-GRADE ALIEN SERIES!

Sixth-Grade Alien
I Shrank My Teacher
Missing — One Brain!
Lunch Swap Disaster
Zombies of the Science Fair
Class Pet Catastrophe

SIXTH-GRADE ALIEN

Zombies of the Science Fair

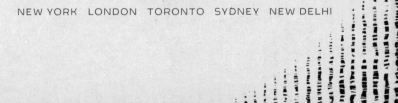

By **BRUCE COVILLE**

Illustrated by Glen Mullaly

ALADDIN

NEW YORK LONDON TORONTO SYDNEY NEW DELHI

ALADDIN

An imprint of Simon & Schuster Children's Publishing Division

1230 Avenue of the Americas, New York, New York 10020

This Aladdin paperback edition October 2020

Text copyright © 2000, 2020 by Bruce Coville

Illustrations copyright © 2020 by Glen Mullaly

Also available in an Aladdin hardcover edition.

All rights reserved, including the right of reproduction in whole or in part in any form.

ALADDIN and related logo are registered trademarks of Simon & Schuster, Inc.

For information about special discounts for bulk purchases, please contact Simon & Schuster Special Sales at 1-866-506-1949 or business@simonandschuster.com.

The Simon & Schuster Speakers Bureau can bring authors to your live event. For more information or to book an event contact the Simon & Schuster Speakers Bureau at 1-866-248-3049 or visit our website at www.simonspeakers.com.

Designed by Tiara Iandiorio

The illustrations for this book were rendered in in a mix of traditional and digital media.

The text of this book was set in Noyh Book.

Manufactured in the United States of America 0820 OFF

2 4 6 8 10 9 7 5 3 1

Library of Congress Control Number 2020938376

ISBN 9781534468054 (hc)

ISBN 9781534468047 (pbk)

ISBN 9781534468061 (eBook)

TABLE OF CONTENTS

CHAPTER 1

[PLESKIT]
A LETTER HOME (TRANSLATION)

FROM: Pleskit Meenom, on the continually puzzling Planet Earth

TO: Maktel Geebrit, on the too distant and deeply longed for Planet Hevi-Hevi

Dear Maktel:

Well, I have caused another uproar here on Earth.

I suspect that this will come as no surprise to you. I guess I'm not surprised myself. But I can't understand it. It's not as if I'm *trying* to cause trouble. It just seems to follow me around.

I ask you—who could have guessed that

a simple project like trying to enhance Tim's brainpower could have turned into the kind of catastrophe I'm about to explain to you?

I've written down the series of events. As usual, Tim helped. I am also including some transmissions written by the being who was one of the reasons so much went wrong with my science fair project. These were retrieved by members of the Trading Patrol after the unfortunate events I am about to describe were all over. If we had been able to get them earlier, it might have saved a great deal of trouble.

There's even a chapter from Linnsy, for reasons you will understand later.

I hope your life is calmer and more quiet than mine.

Are you *ever* going to come to visit?

The Fatherly One sends his regards.

I send this story.

Fremmix Bleeblom!

Your pal,

Pleskit

CHAPTER 2

[TIM]
SCIENCE FAIR BLUES

My head felt as if someone had been hitting it with a sledgehammer. My eyes were burning. My body ached from exhaustion.

"I can't do it!" I cried. "I just can't do it!" My mother sighed. "Can I assume that it's science fair time again?"

I nodded numbly. It was no surprise that my mother was able to figure out my symptoms. This happened to me every year when it came time for the science fair. I longed, ached, yearned to produce the greatest science fair project the school (the school? Heck, the *world!*) had ever seen. I planned and I schemed. I came up with great ideas, projects that would make every kid in the school writhe in envy.

Then reality would set in. The stuff I needed cost too much money. I couldn't find the right books. My idea wasn't realistic anyway. (As my mother is fond of saying, "If they can't solve cold fusion in a multibillion-dollar lab, what makes you think you can do it in my kitchen?")

Most of all, I just didn't have time to pull it all together.

My upstairs neighbor, Linnsy, liked to point out that the main reason I didn't have time to do what I wanted was that I never actually started my project until the night before it was due.

"I don't think a real friend would grind that in," I grumbled.

"If I wasn't your friend I wouldn't take the emotional risk of pointing out your shortcomings," she replied calmly.

"What risk?"

She shrugged. "You might take it badly. You might get angry with me."

"Hah!"

The reason I said "Hah!" is that Linnsy mostly seems to find it amusing when I get mad—which only makes me madder, which only makes her more amused. So it seemed to me the emotional risk was all on my side.

But back to my mother. "What, exactly, is it that you're trying to do?" she asked gently, gazing at the jumble of small metal parts scattered across the kitchen table.

"Robotic squirrel," I muttered.

"Oh, Tim," she sighed. She picked up the remote control for the television, which I had been about to disassemble, and slipped it into her pocket. Obviously, she didn't trust me to return it in working condition. "Why can't you choose a reasonable project for once?"

"Because I'm not a reasonable person!" I cried. "You always tell me I should think big, follow my dreams, believe in myself! Then when I do, you tell me to be reasonable! Ack! Gack! P-tooie!"

Mom sighed again. "My sister warned me about having children. But did I listen? Nooooo. Like an idiot, I went right ahead and had one anyway."

"Ha very ha."

She knelt beside my chair. "Okay, Tim. Let's see what we can do about this. When is the project due?"

"Thursday."

She closed her eyes, and her face looked pained. "Thursday of what week?"

"This one."

She made an obvious effort not to scream. "But that's only two days away!"

"I hope you don't consider that a news flash, Mom."

She groaned. "Tim, how could you possibly have waited this long to start? Especially after what happened last year? And the year before, now that I think of it."

"Hey, those other times I didn't start until the night before the project was due. This time I've got two whole days. Don't I get credit for improvement?"

Ignoring the question, she said, "How did I not know this was happening? How did I not know you were supposed to be getting ready for this?"

"Been working too hard?" I suggested, hoping to distract her with guilt.

"Been not getting messages that were sent home from school because unreliable son failed to deliver them?" she countered.

"They're around," I said, but even I knew that sounded lame.

After that, neither of us said anything for a minute. I could tell she was trying not to get too mad. I was struggling not to do any of *several* stupid things I felt like doing, including (a) screaming, (b) sweeping the entire miserable mess onto the floor, and (c) bursting into tears. Managing to avoid all those, I did something worse instead. My voice dripping bitterness, I said, "I wish Dad was here."

My mother sucked in her breath, and I cursed my fat mouth. "Sorry," I whispered.

She shook her head, and I could see that she didn't trust herself to speak. She stood up, walked to the door, stopped, turned back, turned away, turned back again. "We'll talk later," she said, her voice soft. "I'm sorry, Tim."

Great. Tim Tompkins, emotional genius, strikes again.

I stared at the mess on the table for a while. Finally I decided there was only one thing to do.

I went to my room and sat down at my desk. In front of me was a weird device. Its circular base was about an inch high and maybe eight or nine inches across. Rising from this base was a round screen, about ten inches across and no thicker than a penny. On the base was a single rounded button, purple.

I pushed the button. The screen began to glow. A pair of small boxes folded out from the base. A metallic tentacle stretched up from each of the boxes.

"With whom do you wish to be connected?" asked a pleasant voice.

"Pleskit."

"Noted and logged. I will let you know when contact is established."

I stared at the screen, which was showing a swirling design. After less than a minute the design flickered and was replaced by the familiar purple face of my best friend, Pleskit Meenom, first alien kid to openly go to school on Earth.

CHAPTER 3

[PLESKIT]
SCIENCE FAIR BLUES, PART 2

Barvgis belched contentedly. "That was splendid, Shhh-foop," he said, holding up his bowl. "May I have some more?"

Shhh-foop slid across the floor, her orange tentacles waving delicately. "More *yertztikkia* for the pleasingly round Barvgis coming quickly," she sang. Shhh-foop loves feeding people — I suppose that's why she became a cook to begin with — and I could tell from the trill in her voice that she was happy.

She turned to my bodyguard, Robert McNally. "And perhaps some more for the handsome Just

McNally?" she warbled, using the name that she had become convinced he preferred.

His eyes unreadable behind his sunglasses, McNally shook his head. "No, thanks, Shhh-foop. I've had enough."

I suspected that what he really meant was he had had all he could handle, and would soon be sneaking off to his room for a little snack of Earthling food — possibly some peanut butter, the strange substance that had caused so much trouble when it turned out to make me wildly romantic.

"I wish *I* could have some *yertztikkia*," the Grandfatherly One sighed mournfully.

He couldn't, of course, because he died years ago and has no way to digest food. All we have left of him is his brain, which the Fatherly One kept so that we can have the benefit of his advice and wisdom.

("Not that your Fatherly One ever actually bothers to talk to me," the Grandfatherly One complains every time I see him.)

Normally the Grandfatherly One stays in a large vat in his own room. But earlier that afternoon I had shifted him into his portable Brain Transport Device so he could consult with the rest of us while we were at the table.

Zombies of the Science Fair

It would have been nice to have the advice of the Fatherly One as well, of course. But, as usual, he was off on some important business. I think he was visiting the Queen of England, or someone like that.

Shhh-foop slid back to the counter to fetch the *yertztikkia* for Barvgis. She had not asked if I wanted more, probably because she knows I cannot stand the stuff. It looks as if it were scraped from the bottom of a stagnant pond in the northern wampfields. Smells that way, too.

"So, what's on your mind, Pleskit?" asked Barvgis, licking some *yertztikkia* from the corner of his mouth.

"I am having a terrible time with my project for the science fair," I said, trying not to let my despair sound in my voice.

"Isn't that due on Thursday?" asked a cold, disapproving voice from the doorway. The voice belonged to Ms. Buttsman, who had been assigned by the government of our host country to act as protocol officer for our mission after the disastrous events of our first week on Earth. According to McNally, she knows everything about how to behave properly, and nothing about how to behave pleasantly. Tim calls her "the Butt." I personally

11

think of her as "the dreaded Ms. Buttsman."

"Yes, it is," I replied.

She gave me a sharp, cold smile. "Aren't you a little late starting it?"

Zombies of the Science Fair

I smiled right back at her. "I've already completed three projects, Ms. Buttsman. I'm just not satisfied that any of them is good enough."

Ms. Buttsman's smile faded. "Oh," she said quietly. She turned and walked away from the room.

McNally snorted and gave me that strange Earthling gesture called a high five. "Score one for the Plesman," he said happily. "I do love to see that look on Ms. Buttsman's face."

"I am glad to have been of service, McNally," I said, quite truthfully. "But it does not solve my current problem."

"What are the projects you've done already?" asked Barvgis.

"Well, first I did an analysis of the wave frequencies of Beezle Whompis." Beezle Whompis is the Fatherly One's new assistant. I like him a great deal, even though he is an energy creature and has no actual body.

"Sounds good to me," said McNally.

"I thought so, too," I replied. "Only when I showed it to Ms. Weintraub, she said she thought no one would understand it."

"So what did you do next?" asked the Grand-fatherly One.

"A study of the effect of six different Hevi-Hevian fertilizers on various Earth vegetables."

"So that's where that fifty-pound tomato came from!" cried McNally.

I nodded. "Also the onion the size of my head. Unfortunately, when I showed that project to the Fatherly One, he informed me the plant foods I used are embargoed technology, and I am not allowed to share them with the Earthlings."

"Bummer," said McNally.

"I agree. Then I had a real brainstorm. I did a photo essay on the mating habits of the Veeblax. However, when I showed that project to Ms. Weintraub, she said it was too controversial and was apt to get the entire science fair closed down."

"You've been censored!" cried McNally indignantly.

"Yes, although I do not understand how simple bio-logical facts can be controversial. I considered lodging a formal protest, but the Fatherly One talked me out of it."

McNally nodded. "Probably just as well. You weren't going far with that one."

"But all these dead ends leave me with nothing!" I said unhappily. "I have done three complete projects but still have nothing to take to the science fair. I wish —"

I was interrupted by one of the overhead speakers, which made a belching sound to attract our attention. A mellow voice said, "Pleskit, incoming call on your comm device."

"Who is it?" I asked.

"Your friend Timothy."

"Better take it," said McNally. "Knowing the Timster, he's probably got his butt in trouble again."

In this McNally was correct. When I entered my room and turned on the comm device, I saw that Tim's face looked deeply troubled. His voice sounding as desperate as the expression on his face, he said, "Pleskit, I need your help!"

"What's wrong?" I cried. "Has some evil being kidnapped your mother? Have you accidentally picked up an alien parasite that is slowly gnawing your innards?"

Tim stared at me in horror. "Is that possible?"

"I don't know. I'm just trying to figure out what could have you so upset."

He glanced from side to side, as if embarrassed, then muttered, "I haven't started my project for the science fair yet."

"You mean, you don't like any of the projects you've already finished?" I asked, seeking clarification.

Tim looked at me in puzzlement. "I mean I don't *have* anything. Nothing. Nada. Zilch. Bupkis."

I stared at him, feeling twice as astonished as he had just looked. "What have you been doing all this time?"

"Are you my mother or my friend?" he snarled, causing me to back away from the screen in astonishment. I had never heard him speak like that.

"Your friend," I said. "I think."

"Sorry. Didn't mean to snap at you. I'm just under a lot of stress right now. I've been trying to come up with something brilliant, but all I have is a tableful of scrap parts. I feel like my brain has abandoned me."

That was when I had my great idea.

Given my history with great ideas, I should have *krepot geezborkim* right then.

I didn't.

Instead, I invited Tim to come over to the embassy.

Then I farted the small but exuberant fart of glee.

I had just figured out what I wanted to do for my science project!

CHAPTER 4

[TIM]
PLESKIT PROPOSES HIS PROJECT

I love going to the Hevi-Hevian embassy more than anything. I mean, I spent my entire life wanting to meet an alien. Now I get to visit Earth's first openly alien building almost any time I want. It's so cool that sometimes I worry my head will explode if I think about it too much.

It was early evening and still light, so I rode my bike.

The embassy—which looks a lot like a huge flying saucer—dangles from this big hook that rises from the top of one of the highest hills in the city. So it's easy to spot, even from a long way away.

As usual, the grounds were surrounded by tourists

and sightseers. (According to the newspaper, having the aliens headquartered here has done great things for Syracuse's economy.) Fortunately, I didn't have to press my way through the crowd. I stopped at the blue dome that sits about a hundred yards away from the embassy. Even though the guard knows me pretty well by now, he still made me press my hand against the wall for secure identification. But he smiled and greeted me by name, which was something new.

I got into a silvery capsule that scooted me through an underground transport tube, then up into the embassy. Unfortunately, the first person I ran into was the Butt.

"Well, well, well," she said when she saw me. "Here he is, the source of most of Pleskit's problems. Drop by to create another interplanetary incident, Tim?"

"No, ma'am," I said, as politely as I could manage. "I'm here to work on my science project. We're going to try to find a cure for nastiness."

Ms. Buttsman's eyes flashed and her nostrils flared. But all she said was "I'm sure you'll find a way to turn it into a catastrophe. Pleskit is waiting for you in his room."

Zombies of the Science Fair

"Thank you," I said. I considered belching the Hevi-Hevian phrase for parting, which Pleskit has been teaching me, but decided against it.

If the embassy is one of my favorite places in the world (and it is), then Pleskit's room is one of my favorite places in that favorite place — even if it is a little too tidy for my taste. For one thing, his bed is an air mattress. I don't mean a plastic thing you blow up. This mattress is actually made out of air—"thick" air, specially controlled by a molecular shield. It's the best thing in the world for bouncing on. Plus, it only exists when Pleskit summons it, which he does by making the right smell come out of the knob that grows out of the top of his head plus farting a command. When he wants to get rid of the mattress, he just farts another command and it vanishes.

One good thing about this is that the rest of the time he can use the space that would normally be taken up by the bed for doing something else, which makes his room a lot . . . well, *roomier*. Of course, you have to clear the space off before you can actually use the mattress again, but that's not a big problem for Pleskit.

Bruce Coville

He's so tidy I would have guessed he was an alien even if he weren't purple, since I never knew an Earth kid that neat. (My mother swears they actually do exist, but I think that's just a scam she's trying to pull on me.) Two other cool things about Pleskit's room:

1. His toys, which, being from another planet, are always strange and interesting — even if he does keep them all lined up on a shelf.

2. His pet Veeblax. The Veeblax is this utterly cool little shapeshifter that can turn itself into all kinds of stuff — sort of like a three-dimensional chameleon. It's taken me a while to get to know the Veeblax, but I think it's starting to like me.

When I came in, Pleskit and the Veeblax were bouncing on the bed. Pleskit farted a greeting, something he has learned not to do in school, because it annoys the teachers and causes certain snotty kids (namely Jordan Lynch) to pick on him. Besides, his Fatherly One wants everyone in the embassy to speak only Earthling languages while they are on this mission. But in private, Pleskit is teaching me a little Hevi-Hevian. (Unfortunately, my sense of smell is not strong enough to let me really communicate in their language.)

I scrambled onto the bed and bounced with them for a while — being careful not to bounce off the edge, which is easy enough to do, since you can't see it.

"So, are you ready to make a trade?" he asked, doing a bottom bounce that led to a perfect flip.

"What kind of a trade?" I asked, instantly alert and cautious. Pleskit's people are totally into trading; any deal you make they take *very* seriously.

"About our science projects."

"What do you have in mind?"

Pleskit smiled. "I help you with your science project, just as you wanted."

"Yeah?" I said, bouncing up to touch the ceiling. "And in return?"

"You help me with mine."

I bounced off the bed. "How can I help *you*? You've got all kinds of alien superscience at your command. What do you need me for?"

Pleskit bounced down to join me. "Well, it's not so much that I want you to help me with the project," he said. "Actually, I want you to *be* my science project."

"What are you going to do?" I yelped. "Dissect me?"

Zombies of the Science Fair

"Don't be vulgar, Tim," said Pleskit, putting out his arm so the Veeblax—which had temporarily shaped itself into something like a snake—could slither up it. "I don't want to dissect you. I want to make you smarter."

Torn between excitement and terror, I grabbed the sides of my head and stared at Pleskit. "Can you do that?" I cried.

He smiled. "I'm not sure. But it seemed worth a try."

CHAPTER 5

[PLESKIT]
BEEZLE WHOMPIS

Though Tim looked fearful, I could see a kind of hunger in his eyes. "Don't you think that making you smarter would be a worthy science fair project?" I asked.

"Just how do you plan to do this?" asked Tim, ignoring my question.

"I won't know that till I examine your brain. Also, to be really scientific, we'll have to give you a pre-test and a post-test, so we can tell if the project has worked or not."

The Veeblax slithered off my arm and positioned itself in front of Tim. Then it shaped itself like a giant eyeball and stared up at him. This is a trick it has been doing a lot lately — mostly, I think, because it seems to annoy Ms. Buttsman.

"Look," said Tim, "I'm not going to have surgery, and I'm not going to swallow anything." This didn't surprise me. Between the *finnikle-pokta* that gave him a major barfing episode and the monkeyfood we invented a while ago, Tim remains very nervous about non-Earthling food substances.

I sighed. "That does limit my options." When I saw the look on his face, I began to laugh. "Don't worry, Tim! I wasn't really going to feed you anything!"

"All right, then just exactly how *are* you intending to make me smarter?"

"I told you, I don't know yet. I have to do some research first."

"Hey, we don't have much time, Pleskit. The science fair is Thursday. Besides, I don't think the library is even open tonight."

"We have no need to leave the embassy. I'll just tap into the main computer. Our database contains the unabridged *Encyclopedia Galactica* — all thirty-five thousand two hundred and forty-three volumes."

"A thirty-five-thousand-volume encyclopedia?" Tim yelped. "I don't think we have that many books in our entire school library!"

"The fact that your government does not properly support education is not the issue. The point is, we have all the research material we need right here. In addition to the encyclopedia, the computer contains several million volumes of science, history, poetry, literature, mathematics, and joke books."

"Joke books?" asked Tim. He sounded surprised, and a little suspicious.

"According to the Fatherly One, humor is one of the most important aspects of a civilization. He claims you can never truly understand a culture without understanding its jokes."

Tim smiled. "So how are you doing with Earthling jokes?"

"Not very well, I fear. So far the only way I've found that I can get a laugh for certain is with a fart."

"Sure. Farts are always funny."

"That is hard for me to understand. On Hevi-Hevi we use farts in some of our most serious poetry."

Tim snorted. "You're kidding, right?"

Zombies of the Science Fair

I shook my head. "True poets know that a well-tuned fart can be used to express deep tragedy."

"I may use that line on my mother sometime," said Tim. "But let's get back to the science fair. Do you think you can enhance my brain in time so that I can come up with a killer project of my own?"

"I do not want your project to cause any fatalities!" I cried, alarmed at the idea.

Tim rolled his eyes. "It's just an expression, Pleskit. It means . . . oh, a project that will knock their eyes out."

"Well, we've gone from death to blindness," I said. "I suppose that's a step up."

Tim sighed. "You know what I mean!"

I had to admit that he was right. But I also pointed out how extraordinarily violent his language was.

"But everyone talks like that," said Tim.

"And you're surprised that other planets are nervous about opening relations with you?" I asked. I was about to say more but stopped, realizing that I was on the verge of getting in a fight with my best friend. (Not to mention that I was talking about his world in a way that is not approved.) "Come on," I said, eager to change the subject. "Let's get started.

I think Beezle Whompis can help us with the initial testing."

The office of Beezle Whompis is located just outside the office of the Fatherly One. We didn't see Beezle Whompis when we first entered his room. But the air was crackling with a sense of energy, which is usually a good sign that Beezle Whompis is somewhere nearby. Indeed, seconds after we entered the room, we heard a sizzling sound, and he appeared in his chair.

When in physical form, Beezle Whompis is tall and extremely lean. His eyes are enormous — very dark and deep-set. His parchment-yellow skin stretches tightly over his high cheekbones. Three round nostrils in the center of his face are all he has of a nose.

Even though I had been pretty sure he was nearby, I made a startled noise and released the odor of alarm from my *sphen-gnut-ksher*. The way Tim squeaked let me know that I wasn't the only one who had been surprised. (Or, possibly, that he was bothered by the odor.)

"Sorry, boys," said Beezle Whompis. "Holding on to this shape is a bit of a job, and I like to take a rest in my natural form every now and then. How can I help you?"

"We want to test Tim's intelligence," I said.

Beezle Whompis laughed, a harsh, crackling sound that Tim says always makes him think of radio static. "Why in the world would you want to do that?"

We explained the situation.

"Ah, well, that should be amusing," he said, nodding solemnly.

"Amusing?" asked Tim. He sounded offended.

"Being easily amused is a great gift," said Beezle Whompis. "It makes life vastly more pleasant. Come on, I'll take you to the lab, and we'll see what we can do."

I had been nervous about Beezle Whompis before he arrived, since whoever holds the job of assistant to the Fatherly One can have a great impact on my life. But he was turning out to be one of the best assistants in a long time — partly because he actually seemed to enjoy helping Tim and me with our ideas.

"Follow me," he said, disappearing from where he stood beside his desk and rematerializing at the door.

I had been expecting Beezle Whompis to take us to the embassy lab. He did lead us up to that floor, but instead of the lab we went into another room, one that was mostly white, with a table in the middle. Above the table hung a wide lamp.

"Oh, no!" said Tim, when he saw the table. "I'm not getting up on that thing!"

"No one asked you to," said Beezle Whompis patiently. "Have a seat, please."

Several chairs stood against one of the side walls. Tim and I sat down. Beezle Whompis opened a cupboard and took out a purple box covered with knobs, dials, buttons, gauges, speakers, and antennae. He carried it over to where we sat. Before either of us could say a word, he plunked it down on Tim's head. Though the bottom of the box had appeared solid, his head disappeared inside the thing as it settled all the way to his shoulders.

CHAPTER 6

[TIM]
TESTING, TESTING . . .

When Beezle Whompis stuck that testing box onto my head I felt a moment of total terror. It was pitch-black inside—so dark I felt as if I had fallen into a coal mine. Even worse, the moment the box was in position, my head started to tingle. The tingling didn't really hurt; it was sort of a cross between the pins-and-needles feeling you get when you've sat on your foot too long and the way a barber's clippers feel against your neck. But it was very startling.

"Take it off!" I shouted. But the words sounded muffled, even to me, and I had no idea whether Beezle Whompis and Pleskit could hear me or not.

Bruce Coville

Beezle Whompis said, "Count to ten, Tim." *His* voice was perfectly clear.

I did as he told me, thinking that when I got to ten, he would take the box off me. He didn't. Instead, he gave me a new order: "Imagine the color blue."

By now I was feeling so cranky that I wanted to refuse. But somehow as soon as he told me to do it, my mind called up blue anyway.

Next he told me to state my name and address. Then he had me make a fist. Finally he asked me to imagine what it would be like to have wings. I was just getting into a cool flying fantasy when he took the box off my head.

"What was that all about?" I demanded as soon as my head was in the open.

"What was what all about?" asked Beezle Whompis calmly.

"All those weird questions."

"I was trying to stimulate different areas of your brain so I could get a more accurate reading of your mental activity."

That sounded so interesting I forgot about being angry. "What did you find out?"

"Not much. The activity was too low to register on the dials. Just kidding, just kidding!" he added quickly when he saw the look on my face. "We certainly got enough information to give Pleskit a baseline for his experiment."

"So what's my score?" I asked, both excited and

nervous at finding out how intelligent I was.

Beezle Whompis barked out his staticky crackle of a laugh. "The idea of applying a single score to intelligence is very primitive, Tim. The brain has many functions, many skills. That was why I had you thinking and doing all those different things while the test box was on your head — so I could measure the activity of different areas of your brain. To try to express your brain's capacity in all those different areas with a single number is just plain silly."

"Oh," I said, feeling a little disappointed. "Well, can you give me a general sense of how I did?"

"On the GISMAT comparative scale of intelligent beings you rank somewhere around a two."

"Two?" I shrieked. "That makes me stupider than broccoli!"

Beezle Whompis made his radio-on-the-wrong-channel chuckle. "That depends on the scale you're using. This particular scale goes from one to ten thousand. However, over two dozen advanced civilizations have been developed by beings still at the one level.

"Now, here's another bit of information, one I found quite fascinating. Among the things I tested is something that might be called 'untapped potential.' As it turns out, you are only using a fraction of your brain. This is in line with other research that has been done regarding your species. This issue of untapped potential is one of the things that has made Earth so fascinating to starfarers for some centuries now. How is it that you beings can *have* so much brainpower, and yet use so little of it? A most intriguing question."

Pleskit, who was sitting at a screen examining the data, spoke up. "This is causing me to rethink my project, Beezle Whompis. What if rather than trying to increase Tim's intelligence I simply try to improve his ability to use the brainpower he already has?"

Beezle Whompis flickered around the edges, as if he were about to let go of his physical shape. I decided this must mean he was thinking extra hard. "Interesting idea," he said at last. "The task might be more manageable, yet the final result should be about the same. Why don't you study these readouts and see what you can come up with?"

With that he sizzled out of sight. At first I couldn't tell if he had left the room or just returned to his energy state. But after a minute I could sense a difference in the air that let me know he had gone.

I turned to Pleskit. "So," I said, still feeling a little nervous, "what do you have in mind?"

"I'm not sure. Give me a little while to do some research."

He was sitting at a console, pressing buttons and making smells. At first I thought I might read over his shoulder. Then I realized (not surprisingly) that the *Encyclopedia Galactica* was written in alien, so I decided to play with the Veeblax instead. The little guy seemed to be getting used to me, and it was fun to make a face and watch it try to imitate me. I tried doing the Frankenstein walk and was amused when the Veeblax did an almost perfect copy of it.

My laughter must have disturbed Pleskit, because he growled, "Will you two stop fooling around?"

"Yes, Master," I said obediently. But Pleskit was already back in his research, so the sarcasm was wasted.

The Veeblax and I played quietly for a while longer. Then, just when I was in danger of falling asleep on the floor, Pleskit shouted, "By the Seven Moons of Skatwag, I think I've got it! Come on, Tim. Let's go to the supply room."

Zombies of the Science Fair

Startled, I jumped to my feet. Pleskit was holding a list in his hand. With the Veeblax yeeping and yipping behind us, we hurried down the hall to a room filled with a huge assortment of interesting-looking equipment. Pleskit handed me a box — not a cardboard box, of course, this was made of some purple material and was so light the whole box didn't weigh any more than a cracker.

While I held the box, my purple pal began tossing things into it. The stuff all looked vaguely scientific, though none of it looked much like anything I had ever seen on Earth. He kept checking his list and muttering.

Finally, when the box was nearly full, he cried, "That's it. On to the lab!"

This time the Veeblax wrapped itself around his leg. Lugging the box—fairly heavy, now that it was full—I followed him. In the lab he dumped the parts onto a long table and began humming to himself as he worked. Occasionally he would add a fart to his song, though whether that was for rhythm or for emotional emphasis I couldn't tell.

I started to get worried. "Pleskit, I'm going to have to go home soon."

"That's all right," he muttered. "I'm almost finished."

I wasn't sure he had actually heard me. But not more than ten minutes later he stood back from the bench and cried, "Behold the key to unlocking the potential of Earthly brains!"

"*That* thing's going to make me a genius?" I asked in dismay.

CHAPTER 7

[PLESKIT]
THE POWER OF SUGGESTION

After working so hard on a way to enhance Tim's mental abilities, I was somewhat offended by his reaction to my device, which I had already begun to think of as the "Pleskonian Suggestibility Stimulator."

"What's wrong with it?" I asked.

"It looks like a ray gun!"

"Well, it *is* a ray gun! It's going to send a 'Suggestibility Ray' into your skull. Then, when you are more open to suggestion, I will urge you to use your brain more effectively—thereby releasing your true natural potential. *Krepotzim!* You're smarter. That was the whole point of this, remember?"

"I dunno," said Tim. "It reminds me of the thing Captain Lance Driscoll used on *Tarbox Moon Warriors* to immobilize evil alien beings."

"Tim, when will you accept the fact that *Tarbox Moon Warriors* was just a show? This is reality. Now, shall we go forward with this experiment or not?"

"Shouldn't we test it on something else first? Like, maybe the Veeblax?"

"As far as we know, the Veeblax is already using its brain at full capacity."

Tim sighed. "All right. Give me your best shot."

"I'm not going to shoot you, I'm going to zap you. It's an entirely different thing."

I turned on the ray gun. It made a high-pitched whine as it warmed up. The sound was incredibly annoying. Fortunately, it stopped once the beam was ready. I flipped the switch. Instantly a purple ray surrounded Tim's head. I counted to thirty, then turned off the ray.

Tim sat there, just staring at me. He looked a little *gib-stikkle*. "Is that all?" he asked at last.

"How do you feel?" I replied.

He paused, then said, "How do you want me to feel?"

Zombies of the Science Fair

I blinked. This was not a Tim-like response. On a hunch, I said, "I think you should feel terrific."

"Then I do!" cried Tim, leaping to his feet. "I haven't felt this good in years. It's like I've got raw health pulsing through my veins!"

Clearly, the Suggestibility Ray had worked!

"I bet you feel smarter, too, don't you?" I asked.

Tim paused for a moment. I could almost see his brain readjusting itself. Then he smiled broadly and said, "Boy, you're not kidding. I feel as if I've got brainpower to spare."

Of course, just feeling that way was not enough to prove he really was smarter— or, to be more precise, that he was actually using more of his usually untapped intelligence.

I remembered a math lesson we had had earlier in the week, and the trouble Tim had had with multiplying fractions.

"What's three-fifths times seven-twelfths?" I asked.

Tim paused, looked at me oddly, then said, "It's twenty-one over sixty, which reduces to seven-twentieths. Very close to being one-third, of course, if you're just looking for a quick approximation. Or, you could do it in decimals, which would be .6 times .58333 — I'm stopping at five places, since the threes would actually go on forever—which works out to be .349998."

The ray had *definitely* worked.

"Come on," I said. "Let's go show Beezle Whompis."

"Whatever you want," replied Tim placidly.

It didn't take long to find the Fatherly One's assistant, since he was at his regular station in front of the Fatherly One's office.

"We need to give Tim the post-test now," I said.

Beezle Whompis looked a little startled. "That was fast!"

I emitted the spicy smell of pride from my *sphen-gnut-ksher* and said, "When you're hot you're hot."

Beezle Whompis looked puzzled.

"It's an Earthling expression," I explained.

"Not one of overwhelming modesty, I take it," said Beezle Whompis.

I lowered my head. "Forgive me if I am too exuberant. I am excited about this project."

"How do *you* feel about it?" asked Beezle Whompis,

turning to Tim, who had stood without speaking all this time.

His eyes got wide and he shrieked, "I'm excited, too!"

Beezle Whompis flickered a little around the edges. "All right, let's go do a test."

The results of the second test were interesting, but a little puzzling. Though Tim's brain was obviously functioning at a much higher level now — "*Startlingly* higher," according to Beezle Whompis — there were some odd bobbles in the test results, including a few areas where the brain activity had actually been depressed a bit.

"This is going to take further study," said Beezle Whompis.

"It certainly is," agreed Tim. "Also, if you are going to have an effective project, Pleskit, then I think you need to do some additional testing. The numbers on this GISMAT scale of yours will not mean much to the judges. You need something more concrete, like giving me some math and spelling tests before and after a treatment with the ray."

I looked at Tim in surprise.

He grinned back. "This is fun!"

Beezle Whompis, who was looking slightly worried, said, "Let me try something, Pleskit."

"All right," I said, wondering what he had in mind.

Turning to Tim, Beezle Whompis said, "I think you're feeling a bit sleepy now, Tim. Don't you? In fact, I bet you'd like to take a little rest."

Tim paused, thought for a moment, then said, "I don't think so. In fact, I feel really wide awake."

"Well, that's a relief," said Beezle Whompis.

"What is?" I asked.

"It appears Tim's suggestibility is limited to whoever actually used the ray on him." He shook his head, and sparks showed in his noseholes. "I would hate to leave the poor boy wide open to every suggestion that came his way. The commercials he'd see in just an hour of Earthly television would probably cause him to short-circuit!"

"I hadn't thought of that," I said nervously.

"I had," said Tim.

"Well, why didn't you mention it?" I asked, somewhat crossly.

"You didn't ask."

I decided I was glad the ray was scheduled to wear

off at midnight. But it was important that Tim get some use out of it before it was gone.

"I think you should go home now," I said gently. "I have a strong feeling that you want to work on your project. In fact, I think you're going to be amazed at what a good job you do. It will probably be brilliant!"

"Sounds like a good idea to me," said Tim. "In fact, I feel inspired!"

Just for safety, we decided to have McNally escort Tim home. We were pretty sure his suggestibility was limited to comments that came from me. Even so, we didn't want to take any chances.

CHAPTER 8

[TIM]
FROM RAY GUN TO SPRAY GUN

When Pleskit zapped me with the Suggestibility Ray, at first I didn't think anything had happened. The only difference I noticed was that I felt a little more calm and quiet than usual—also, a little like I was waiting for something.

But when he suggested I was feeling terrific, it was as if someone had flipped a switch in my body and given me a jolt of pure health. I felt I could climb a mountain, swim an ocean, wrestle a tiger—all at the same time and with one hand tied behind my back!

It was the same way when he suggested I was feeling smarter; I could almost *feel* my brain heating up. It was as if my head were a big old house where a lot of the rooms had been closed off for years, and all of a sudden the doors were being flung open, and fresh air and sunshine were flooding in. It was great—except I didn't know what to do with it, until Pleskit asked me that question about fractions, which was so simple it was almost insulting.

All the time that McNally and Ralph-the-driver were taking me home, I was thinking about possible science fair projects—and thinking clearly, quickly discarding things I knew I couldn't do, even with my enhanced ability. Not only did my project have to be reasonable, it had to be something I could reasonably pull off by two A.M. Thursday morning, which was about the point that I knew I would totally run out of steam and collapse if I was trying to work really late.

I was thinking so hard, I scarcely noticed when we pulled up in front of the apartment building, until McNally said, "Here you go, Tim. Wait a sec, while I pull your bike out of the trunk."

When I went into the apartment, my mother was in the bathroom. She had a small plastic bottle stuck up her

47

nose. She gave it a little squeeze. "Ah!" she sighed. "That's better. I feel like I can breathe again." She turned to me. "How'd you make out over at Pleskit's, hon?"

"Fine. I think I may actually be able to get a science project done after all."

She put her hand to her chest and staggered backward. "Will this be the year my dreams come true?" she cried.

"You should audition for Comedy Central, Mom. I hear they're willing to take even the really pathetic acts."

She rolled her eyes and turned back to the mirror. "Let me know if I can do anything to help." She picked up a comb and worked at her hair a bit, then used a can of hair spray to shoot some mist at her head.

"And another piece of the ozone layer bites the dust," I said. I was still standing there watching her because an idea was starting to hatch at the back of my brain. I wasn't sure what it was yet, but I wanted to give it a chance to get out of its shell.

Mom snorted. "If you want to talk about saving the environment, let's start with that toxic waste dump you call your bedroom. Besides, this spray is environmentally friendly. See?"

Zombies of the Science Fair

She handed me the container. I studied the thing and realized she was right—it was a pump-action spray, no ozone-depleting chemicals.

I thought about the nasal spray she had just used.

The eggshell cracked and the idea rolled out. It was still a little wet, a little groggy, sort of blinking in the sunlight. But at least it had a shape.

"I think I can get a science fair project out of this," I said.

My mother looked skeptical.

"No, really," I said. "Look, you were just using that nasal spray. And here's the pump on this hair spray. I could do a project on all the different ways people spray stuff. I can talk about pressure and velocity and droplet size and propellant techniques and things like that. I can compare things, make some charts—"

My mother was looking at me in astonishment. "Tim, that's actually a reasonable project."

"Well, what did you expect?"

"Based on past experience? Oh, I don't know. A plan to demonstrate do-it-yourself brain surgery. An idea for putting a mouse on the moon. A design for a working time machine. Schemes for nuclear—"

"Mom, I'm serious here. Now, can you help me out with this a bit?"

She looked even more astonished than before. "Sorry, Tim. I didn't mean to be sarcastic. Actually, I think it's a pretty cool idea. I guess the next thing we need to do is figure out how many different ways there are to spray things."

"Okay, that makes sense. Let's get to work."

Half an hour later we had a collection of three dozen cans, bottles, and pumps of various kinds on the kitchen table.

"A lot of these work the same way," said my mother.

"That's all right. I only need four or five different types. We'll check them out and eliminate the duplicates."

Which we did.

I ended up with five things on the table: the bottle of nasal spray, a bottle that worked the same way as the hair-spray pump, another bottle with a kind of trigger that Mom used to squirt water on clothes when she was ironing, a non-ozone-depleting aerosol can, and one of my own squirt guns.

"Not a bad collection," said Mom.

"It's okay. I wish I had one more thing — maybe something older, to show how people used to spray stuff."

"Wait a minute!" cried Mom. She dashed out of the room. I heard her rummaging in the hall closet—which, believe me, is not one bit more organized than my bedroom. "Come on, Tim," she called. "Give me a hand here."

I went into the hall. Mom passed me a box she had just lifted down from the top shelf. Then another, then another.

"Do you want me to open these?" I asked.

"No, just get them out of the way."

"What are we looking for?"

"You'll see," she said, wiggling her eyebrows at me.

I sighed and set the boxes on the floor as she handed them to me.

"Aha!" she cried at last. "Here it is."

She pulled out a box that clanked and clanged. When she put it on the floor and opened it, I could see that it was mostly garden stuff—little hand tools for digging in the dirt. She poked around in it for a minute and pulled out this weird device.

"*Voilà!*" she said, handing it to me.

"What the heck is it?"

"Your grandmother's bug sprayer."

I studied the device. The body of it was a long metal tube about the size of the cardboard tube inside a roll of paper towels. Mounted just under one end of the tube was a can, about twice the size of a can of vegetables, with a screw-off cap on one side. A wooden handle stuck out of the other end of the tube.

"You put your bug spray in here," said Mom, pointing at the cap on the can. "Then you pump with the handle to spray it out. Try it."

I pulled on the handle. A thin rod came out through a hole in the end of the tube.

"Now push the handle back in," said Mom.

I did as she said.

"Nothing happens."

"Well, of course not. It's empty. Come on, let's go in the kitchen and fill it with water."

We did as she suggested, first washing the canister out two or three times, to make sure there was no insecticide left in it.

"Okay, now give it a try," said Mom. "Here, I'll open the window."

I pointed the spray gun at the window and pushed on the rod. A mist came shooting out from the other end.

Zombies of the Science Fair

"Cool!" I said.

"Gramma used to use this in her rose garden," said Mom. "She claimed to have slain thousands of Japanese beetles with it."

I sat down at the table with all my spray devices and began to work. I worked hard and long, convincing my mother to let me stay up way past my bedtime. Then, about midnight, I suddenly felt as if the doors in my head were slamming shut. Five minutes later I was sound asleep, my head on the table, my snores (according to my mother) rattling the windows.

RECOVERED COMMUNICATION (TRANSLATION)

FROM: Skizzdor, just above the backward and barbaric but potentially very profitable Planet Earth

TO: One who must remain nameless

Glorious Leader:

Events have played into our hands quite nicely. It now looks very much as if we will be able to intercept and abduct the ambassador's brat at the time you have suggested.

If we are successful, I will send the signal, and Urkding can swing down with the shuttlecraft to pick up me and the brat. We may have to bring one or two of the Earthling children with us, but that should be a minor inconvenience. We can always jettison them once we are in space.

I await further instructions.

Skizzdor

CHAPTER 9

[PLESKIT]
FAIR CHANCE

I couldn't wait to see Tim at school the next day so I could find out how he had made out with his science project.

"It was great!" he said enthusiastically. "At least, until the Suggestibility Ray wore off. Then I crashed big-time."

"Did you hurt yourself?" I asked, deeply concerned. I did not want to have been the cause of an accident.

Tim rolled his eyes. "It's just an expression, Pleskit. It means I ran out of energy and fell asleep."

"Oh. Well, that's all right. Sleep is our friend. It is nature's way of restoring our strength. It is —"

Zombies of the Science Fair

Tim began to laugh. "You're like a walking science fair all by yourself!"

"I just want to do well at *this* fair," I replied. "I have made so many messes in such a short time, it would be nice to have something go right for a change. But I think I am in good shape with this project. However, we will need to give you another dose of the Suggestibility Ray tonight for me to complete my research and measurements."

"That's fine with me! I'm going to need to have my brain running at top speed to finish my own project—though it would be nice if you could plan on it lasting a little longer this time. Last night it wore off at midnight, and tonight I'll need to work until at least two in the morning." He paused, then said, "Actually, maybe I won't need to do that if I'm as smart as I was last night. But working until two on the night before the science fair is sort of a tradition for me, so I'd just as soon be prepared for it."

"I'll see what I can do," I promised.

"Class. Class! I want you to come to order now!" called Ms. Weintraub.

Once we were all in our seats, she began asking how people were doing with their science fair projects.

"Remember, we'll be setting up in the gym tomorrow afternoon, and I hope you'll all have something that will make me proud of you. I know most of you are in good shape. Tim, I'm concerned because I haven't seen much on your project yet."

This comment caused a number of laughs and snickers from around the room.

"I changed topics again," said Tim.

Ms. Weintraub groaned.

"No, no, it's gonna be fine!" said Tim quickly. "I'm doing a report on how different types of spraying mechanisms work."

Ms. Weintraub blinked. "That's a remarkably subdued topic for you, Tim."

"Subdued, but *doable*," he replied. "I finally got that part figured out."

"What a brainstorm," said Jordan Lynch, who never missed an opportunity to tease Tim.

"And I suppose yours is all finished, Jordan?" asked Ms. Weintraub.

"Almost," said Jordan cautiously. "I still have to get a couple more computer parts, but they're supposed to come in today."

Zombies of the Science Fair

Tim leaned over to me and whispered, "Translation: Some poor guy who works for Jordan's father is going to finish the project for him today."

I looked at him in shock.

"Trust me," said Tim. "Science fair projects are not the kind of thing Jordan does on his own."

Ms. Weintraub saw us whispering and said, "How about you, Pleskit? Have you settled on a topic yet? I would be more concerned if I didn't know how fast you can do one of these projects. But really, you do have to make a choice."

I smiled at her. "I'm working on a project to be called 'A Study of Free Will and Intelligence in the Human Organism.' I think you will find it very interesting."

"That's odd," said Larrabe Hicks. "Mine is called 'Free Will and Intelligence in Woodchucks'!"

"Nature boy strikes again," muttered Jordan.

After school that afternoon McNally and Ralph-the-driver took us to Tim's apartment to pick up the materials for his science fair project. Then we came back to the embassy. After Shhh-foop had given us a little snack (which Tim hardly touched!), we settled down to work.

"Ready to give me another dose of the brain ray?" Tim asked eagerly.

I shook my head. "I want to make some adjustments to it first."

"I hope it won't take too long," said Tim uneasily. "I've still got a lot to do on my project, and I'd rather do it with my brain in high gear!"

"Just a few minutes," I said, scooping the Veeblax off the counter and handing it to Tim. "I want to add a device so I can control the strength of the ray. It shouldn't take me long."

While Tim amused himself by trying to get the Veeblax to imitate a cat—he had brought some photos with him for just that purpose—I worked on the Suggestibility Ray. It didn't take long to add the adjustor. When I was ready, I called Tim over and gave him an extra-strength dose of the ray.

"I bet you're feeling good," I said when I was done.

"I feel terrific!" he cried.

"Good. I have the impression you're feeling terrifically intelligent, too. Why don't you get busy on your project for the science fair. I bet you're going to have fun working on it."

Zombies of the Science Fair

"You're not kidding!" cried Tim. "I love this stuff!"

Pushing up his sleeves, he sat down in front of one of the counters and began doing calculations, drawing graphs, and making labels for illustrations he had already stuck on a display board.

I continued working on my project as well, designing an animated demonstration of the human brain. Soon I was deep into the work, so absorbed I forgot about eating. Even so, I was aware of the skritch of Tim's pencil, the sound of his scissors cutting paper, the farty noise of the glue bottle when he squeezed out glue.

I'm not sure when I noticed that the room had fallen silent.

I turned around. Tim's project was finished. It looked very impressive.

Tim, however, did not. He was sitting in front of the display, staring at it with a blank expression on his face.

"Are you all right, Tim?" I asked anxiously.

"I don't know," he said. "Am I?"

I began to feel nervous. "Why aren't you moving?"

His answer sent a thrill of terror tingling through my *sphen-gnut-ksher*. Looking at me with vacant eyes, he said, "I'm waiting for you to tell me what to do next."

CHAPTER 10

[TIM]
THE NEW ME

It is hard for me to explain how I felt as I sat there in front of my science project. My brain was sharp and clear, ready for action. But my energy . . . well, I didn't feel any energy at all. It was as if a switch had been turned off inside me. Even though I had a vague sense of being hungry, I had no urge to do anything but sit and wait for my next suggestion from Pleskit.

I could tell from the rotting carp smell that came from his *sphen-gnut-ksher* that he was upset. "Tim!" he said urgently. "Tim, talk to me!"

"Certainly," I replied, glad to oblige. "What do you want me to talk about?"

"Uh . . . *Tarbox Moon Warriors!*"

"Certainly," I said again, and began to recite the show's description from *Ballon's Guide to Classic Television Sci-Fi.* "*Tarbox Moon Warriors* was one of the great science-fiction shows of early television. The crew of the Tarbox consisted of the strong and heroic captain Lance Driscoll, his wisecracking pilot, Hunter Wilbourne, known for—"

"Stop!" cried Pleskit.

"All right."

"Don't you want to know why I told you to stop?" he asked, sounding almost terrified.

"If you want to tell me."

"No, I want *you* to *want* to know."

"Well, in that case, I'm dying to find out!" I cried, filled with a sudden, desperate longing to know exactly that.

"Are you serious?" asked Pleskit suspiciously.

"As serious as you want me to be."

"*Gibblespratten,*" muttered Pleskit, which confused me, since I had no idea *what* I was supposed to think. Pleskit stared at me for a minute, tapping his nose. He took a deep breath, then said, "I think it's time you were your old self again, don't you, Tim?"

It was as if some strange fog had lifted from my brain. I shook my head, blinked a couple of times, then said, "What the heck was *that* all about?"

"I fear the Suggestibility Ray was more successful than I intended," said Pleskit. "It took away your free will, leaving you in a state where you would not do anything unless I suggested it."

"Whoa," I said nervously. "I don't like the sound of *that!*"

"It was certainly not my intention when I started this project," said Pleskit. "On the other hand, it is an interesting development. Perhaps it will make my science fair project more compelling."

I looked at my own project. Though I could hardly remember having worked on it, it looked pretty good — better than anything I had ever managed before. And it was only eight o'clock. A new record!

"Look," I said nervously, "am I back to normal now, or is the Suggestibility Ray still in effect?"

Pleskit wrinkled his brow, and his *sphen-gnut-ksher* bent sideways. "I'm not sure. I suggested you should be back to normal, but I don't know if that erased the effect of the ray, or if the thing is still in effect underneath your seeming normalcy. It shouldn't make that much difference. Your suggestibility was limited to things I said, so it's not like anyone else can suggest something weird."

"Good thing I trust you," I said.

"And a good thing that the science fair is tomorrow," said Pleskit. "I don't think we should use this thing anymore."

I sighed. "You're probably right. But I'm going to miss being a genius."

"The intelligence remains," said Pleskit. "You just can't get at it. Of course, that seems to be one of the basic problems of the human race."

Mom was astonished when I arrived home from the embassy with my project completed and ready to go.

"Is this really my son?" she asked.

"Yeah, pretty much," I said, not wanting to get into details.

I chowed down hard, then headed for bed. As I drifted off, it occurred to me that, of all the strange things that had happened in the last few days, getting a decent night's sleep before the science fair was probably the strangest.

* * *

The next morning Mom drove me and Linnsy — and our science fair projects — to school. Linnsy's project had involved growing several kinds of mold on different foods. Obviously, she had started it way back when we were supposed to.

School wasn't bad that day, though the time seemed to drag because all I could think about was going to the gym to set up our projects. Classes were scheduled to go in one at a time, so things wouldn't get too crowded and crazy. Our class was supposed to go in right after lunch. Normally, I dreaded the setup, since that was when I finally had to display how little I had actually done. But this year I was so excited by the fact that I had my project finished that I couldn't wait to get going.

But I had to, of course. Sometimes I get the feeling that the biggest thing they're trying to teach us in school isn't reading, writing, or math.

It's waiting.

After about five hundred years had passed, it was our turn to set up. We gathered our projects — which had been taking up all the available space in our room — and headed down the hall.

Zombies of the Science Fair

Several classes had already set up their displays, of course. Unfortunately, this made it hard for me to focus on my own work, since I kept wanting to go look at what the other kids had done.

Pleskit and I worked side by side. His display was incredible. It had three-dimensional holographic X-rays of the brain of his "anonymous subject" (Mr. Anonymous being me, of course), computer simulations of how various parts of the brain worked, charts about suggestibility, and an explanation of how the brain-testing was done to begin with. The centerpiece of the display was the "Pleskonian Suggestibility Stimulator" (his fancy name for the Suggestibility Ray), which Pleskit had now equipped with a safety switch so that no one would turn it on by accident.

Next to all that, my display looked fairly pathetic—though I was still proud to have one at all for a change. Several kids complimented me on it, which made me feel good. And everyone seemed to get a kick out of Gramma's old spray gun.

Jordan's display was on computer graphics. It was very impressive. But I don't think he had any idea of what was really in it.

Larrabe's woodchuck display was kind of cute. Linnsy's mold project looked totally professional (and unlike Jordan, she had done it all on her own). Misty Longacres had a neat project on plant growth and soil types. And Michael Wu had done a very cool project on simple tools, which had been one of our first units that year. The coolest part was a big galvanized tub connected to a set of pulleys that he wanted to connect to the ceiling so he could demonstrate how he could hoist himself into the air. Unfortunately, the ceiling in the gym was way too high for that. Finally Principal Grand and Coach Philgrinn agreed to let him hook it to one of the metal bars holding up the basketball backboard.

After we were pretty much set up, I was talking to Linnsy when Jordan came ambling by. Brad Kent, Jordan's deputy butthead, was with him. No surprise there. Brad follows Jordan like stink follows a skunk.

They stopped to stare at my project.

"Methods of Spraying?" said Jordan in disbelief. "Man, you give new meaning to the word 'lame,' Tompkins!"

"Hey, at least I made this myself, rather than having my father buy it for me," I shot back.

Zombies of the Science Fair

He narrowed his eyes, then snarled, "Hey, at least I've *got* a father."

It would have been easier if he had just hit me — though in a way it was like being hit, since I actually staggered under the insult. Other than that, I couldn't move. I felt as if I were frozen.

Linnsy stepped between us. She's as tall as Jordan, and plenty tough when she wants to be. "That's enough, Jordan," she said, her voice low but firm. "Get your sorry butt out of here."

Jordan stared at her for a moment, then shrugged. "Good thing you've got a *girl* to protect you, Tompkins," he sneered, making "girl" sound like a dirty word. He

and Brad turned and swaggered away, laughing as they went.

I wanted to thank Linnsy, but I was too upset and embarrassed to say anything.

Even more, I wanted the strength and the wit to be able to strike back at Jordan.

And I knew where to get it.

Stepping to Pleskit's display, I grabbed the ray gun.

"Tim!" cried Linnsy. "Don't!"

Ignoring her frantic attempt to stop me, I flipped the safety switch and turned the ray on myself full force.

CHAPTER 11

[PLESKIT]
THE ZOMBIE

I was at the end of the gym, studying Michael
Wu's pulley project, when Linnsy grabbed my arm and
whispered urgently, "Pleskit! We've got a problem!"

Humans do not communicate by smell. Even so,
they send more information by odor than they realize,
and the strong scent of fear I picked up from Linnsy
made my *clinkus* tighten.

"What is it?" I asked, keeping my voice low as she
had done.

"Just come with me."

Before we even got back to my display, I could see
that whatever the problem was, it involved Tim. He was

standing in front of the table, pointing the Suggestibility Ray directly at his own head.

That was strange enough.

What was even stranger was that he was absolutely motionless.

"What happened?" I asked as we hurried toward him.

"He gave himself a dose of the ray," said Linnsy. "Then he just sort of froze."

"What?" I cried. "Why would he do that?"

Other people turned to look at us. I lowered my voice. "Why would he do that?" I repeated.

"I don't know," said Linnsy. "We had a problem with Jordan — it was pretty nasty, actually — and next thing I knew Tim was pointing the ray at himself."

I glanced around for McNally. He was at the side of the gym, talking to Ms. Weintraub. The other kids were scattered at various tables, either still setting up their own projects or looking at someone else's. No one seemed to have realized what was happening.

I hurried to Tim's side. He stared straight ahead, a glazed expression on his face.

"Tim!" I cried. "Are you all right?"

No answer.

Zombies of the Science Fair

Realizing my mistake, I said suggestively, "You probably feel pretty good."

No answer.

I realized with horror that, since I had not administered this dose of the ray, I was not the one he was bound to take suggestions from!

Desperate, I decided to go for a direct command: "Tim, answer me!"

No answer.

"What's going on?" asked Linnsy. She sounded frightened, which made sense to me, since I was pretty terrified myself.

Concealing my fear, I tried again. Making my voice as stern and commanding as I could without actually shouting, I said, "Tim, take a step forward."

For a moment, there was no response. Then Tim said, "Yes, Master." His voice sounded cold and mechanical. And his movements were stiff as he followed my command. But at least he had moved.

"Pleskit!" cried Linnsy. "You've turned Tim into a zombie!"

"I don't even know what a zombie is," I said, trying to fight down the feeling of terror threatening to throw

me into *kleptra*. "Besides, I didn't do it. He gave himself that last dose of the ray."

I turned to Tim. Using that same firm voice, I said, "Tim, I order you to act like your old self again."

He stood without moving for a moment. Then he started to tremble, almost as if he were trying to do something but couldn't. After a moment or two of this he spoke. The words, when they came, were slow and halting.

"I . . . do . . . not . . . understand."

My *clinkus* got even tighter and felt so cold I could barely breathe. Turning to Linnsy, I said, "Go get McNally. We've got to get Tim back to the embassy so I can work on an antidote."

She nodded. "I'll be right back."

As she left I ordered Tim to walk behind the project so no one would see him.

He hesitated, then shambled forward, not looking from side to side. As he went behind my display, I had a sudden thought. Running after him, I said, "Tim, are you doing this for a joke? If you are, please stop it now."

"I . . . do . . . not . . . understand," he said again.

I poked him. He didn't flinch. I snapped my fingers in front of his eyes. He didn't blink.

My hope that this was a mere prank collapsed.

Before I could think what to do next, McNally appeared beside me. "Holy smoke!" he cried. "What happened to *him*?"

"He's been zombified," said Linnsy, who was standing beside McNally.

"We have to get him back to the embassy," I said. "I need to work on an antidote."

McNally saw the need for immediate action, which meant he would save his questions — and any lecture I might get — for later. He glanced around quickly, then said, "Better if we can get him out of here without attracting a lot of attention. No need to stir up another round of anti-alien hysteria — though if you can't snap him out of this, that's gonna happen anyway."

I groaned. It was not enough that my best friend was now a zombie — whatever that was. I had once again endangered the mission of the Fatherly One. This was a problem not only for us, but for the entire planet, since if the Fatherly One is recalled by the Interplanetary Trading Federation, the next beings who have a claim on Earth are more likely to simply take over the planet than to try developing it as a trading partner.

Zombies of the Science Fair

All I wanted to do was create a science project that would have useful information for Earthlings. Yet once again I had managed to put the entire planet in danger.

Desperate measures were required.

"How are we going to get him out of here without attracting all kinds of attention?" asked McNally.

"How about the box I used to carry my project?" suggested Linnsy.

McNally and I just looked at her.

"I'm serious! You can put Tim in the box and carry him out the side door. I'll go tell Ms. Weintraub that Tim and I are going back to the embassy with you to help Pleskit with an unexpected problem — which is pretty much the truth."

"You don't need to go," said McNally.

"If you want to use my carton, I do," replied Linnsy firmly.

McNally groaned. "I should have listened to my mother and joined the Marines. All right, I don't have time to argue. Go clear things with Weintraub."

"Be right back!" said Linnsy.

"Not here," I said. "Meet us at the side exit."

While Linnsy ran off to talk to Ms. Weintraub, I

retrieved the carton from under the table where she had put up her display and carried it behind my own project.

I looked at the box.

I looked at Tim.

Only one way he was going to fit.

"Squat down!" I ordered.

Without a word, he did as I said.

McNally picked him up and put him in the box. He folded the flaps over him. Then he bent down and picked up the box, grunting a little with the effort.

"Come on, Pleskit," he said. "Let's get out of here."

I followed my bodyguard as he carried the box that held my friend to the side of the gym.

Linnsy met us at the door.

"I sure hope you know what you're doing," she said.

"So do I," I whispered. "So do I."

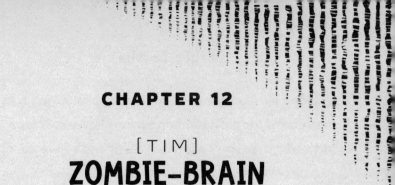

CHAPTER 12

[TIM]
ZOMBIE-BRAIN

All right, you're probably wondering why I zapped myself with the Suggestibility Ray.

First, I was so upset with Jordan that I wasn't thinking entirely straight.

Second, what I *had* thought would happen was that if I kept a suggestion in my mind as I used the ray, the suggestion would still be in place once the ray took hold.

So I told myself, "You are going to be smart and strong!" then blasted myself with a full-strength dose of suggestibility.

My theory was screamingly wrong. As soon as that purple ray hit me, I felt my energy start to slide away. I couldn't move or speak. I had no control of my body. It was one of the most terrifying things I have ever experienced . . . as scary as when Pleskit and I were being held captive by Mikta-makta-mookta and she was going to empty our brains. My brain wasn't empty, but I felt as if the connection between it and my body, it and my willpower, had been severed.

So I just stood there, holding the ray gun, unable to move or speak.

When Pleskit first tried to suggest things to me, nothing happened. By zapping myself I had made myself the Suggester. Only I couldn't suggest anything.

Fortunately, when Pleskit got *very* stern, his orders somehow got through the fog of my brain and I responded to them. My theory is that this worked because he had already used the ray on me a couple of times, and that had some leftover effect.

It was incredibly frustrating to be trapped inside a body I could not control. I knew who I was and what I had been, but it didn't seem to make any difference. Now I was just a zombie, with no willpower, no ability to change anything, to move a muscle on my own.

When Pleskit ordered me to squat, I squatted.

Zombies of the Science Fair

When McNally picked me up and put me in the carton, it didn't really bother me.

That's just the way things were.

McNally closed the box.

It was dark. I felt like I should be afraid, but since no one had told me to, I couldn't manage to summon up the emotion.

McNally picked me up.

I heard a door open, then close behind us.

"That's a relief," said McNally.

"Look!" cried Linnsy. "What's that?"

CHAPTER 13

[LINNSY]
MAD SCIENTIST

First, in case you're wondering why I, Linnsy, am writing this chapter, it's because Tim was packed in a box and Pleskit says he has too little memory of what occurred after he went into his creative frenzy to describe what happened next.

So they asked me to do it.

When we came out the side of the gymnasium, I figured we had made our escape and would just head straight for the embassy. That was before I saw the dark figure lurking at the edge of the building.

What made the figure particularly strange was

82

that it seemed to shimmer around the edges.

"What's that?" I cried.

McNally spun around so fast he nearly dropped the box with Tim inside. "What's what?"

I pointed to where I had seen the figure. "That!"

But it was too late. The figure was gone.

I described what I had seen.

"Great," muttered McNally nervously. "A mysterious stranger. That's all we need. All right, we can't take a chance out here. We'll have to go back inside and try something else."

Which was a good idea, except for one thing. The doors had security locks and couldn't be opened from the outside. And when I peered through the window, I saw our class lining up to leave the gym. I pounded on the door, but it was too late. They were gone.

"Tremendous," fumed McNally. "Just beautiful. All right, let me readjust this." He shifted around so that he had the box with Tim in it on his back. He bent forward so that he was supporting the box mostly with his back and could keep it in place with one hand. Then he reached his other hand inside his jacket and pulled out a gun.

I suppose I shouldn't have been all that surprised.

After all, I knew McNally was a bodyguard, and body-guards have to carry weapons.

Even so, it was a shock to see it.

"Now look," he said grimly. "You two stick with me till we get to the limo. No wandering off!"

We did exactly as he said. I, for one, had no interest in leaving his side.

The limo was parked in the lot at the back of the building. Ralph-the-driver looked at us oddly. But he didn't say anything. According to Tim, he never does.

McNally put the box with Tim in it in the front seat. He fiddled around for a minute, trying to secure it with the seat belt, but finally gave up.

"Drive carefully," he said to Ralph. He didn't explain what was in the box.

Ralph nodded.

McNally, Pleskit, and I climbed into the backseat. It was only the second time I had been in the limo, and I was excited about it. Though I had never told Tim, I was pretty jealous of all the times he got to ride in the limo and go to the embassy. I also think that's one of the reasons Jordan has been on his case even more than usual for the last few weeks. He's really annoyed that

Zombies of the Science Fair

Tim is the one who gets to do all this cool stuff.

When we got close to the hill in Thorncraft Park where the embassy is located, Ralph pushed a button on the dashboard. A door opened in the ground, and we drove down a long ramp. Then we took this slick glass elevator up the "pipe" (as Pleskit called it) into the embassy itself. Instead of getting out at the main reception area, as we had the one other time I was in the embassy, we went to one of the upper levels.

Pleskit led the way to his laboratory. McNally — still lugging the box with Tim inside — came second. I brought up the rear, listening for Ms. Buttsman — though what I was supposed to say if she showed up I have no idea.

In the lab McNally opened the box. Pleskit ordered Tim to stand up.

He did, moving slowly. His face was totally blank. It didn't seem to bother him at all that he had spent the last fifteen minutes folded up in a box.

"Go stand over there," ordered Pleskit, pointing to a spot against the wall.

"Yes, Master," said Tim. He shambled across the floor and stopped at the wall. He was still facing it.

Pleskit sighed. "Turn around!"

"Yes, Master."

"And stop calling me Master!"

"Yes, mmmm . . . mmmm . . . mmmm —"

Tim stopped, obviously uncertain of what to say next.

"You made your best friend into a zombie!" cried McNally. He sounded horrified.

Pleskit made a terrible smell. "Linnsy said the same thing! Just what is a zombie?"

"Someone who has died and been brought back to life by an evil magician who wants to use him as a slave," I said.

"Zgribnick!" cried Pleskit. "Tim has not died, I do not want to use him as a slave, and I am not an evil magician!"

I sighed. "That's just where the word comes from originally," I explained. "I read a book about it last summer. It's pretty cool. These voodoo priests down in Haiti have this special poison made from toads and sea snakes and tarantulas and all kinds of stuff, and they use it to sap a person's will. People used to think it was just a myth, but this guy from Harvard went down there and figured it all out. Anyway, that's where the word comes from. But now it just means someone who moves mindlessly and doesn't seem to have any will of his own."

Pleskit looked at Tim uneasily. "Well, I guess he qualifies. All right, I've got to do something about this. Please do not interrupt me. I must go into major thought mode."

McNally and I sat quietly at the side of the room. Tim, of course, was no trouble at all. Pleskit went to one of the computers and began to work. His fingers flew over the control area, which was sort of like a keypad, but had additional buttons, wheels, and levers, plus a bunch of other things I don't even have names for.

He began to hum. Well, not hum, exactly. It was more of a high-pitched whine. After a while it seemed to be drilling a hole in my head. I wanted to shout for him to stop, only I was afraid of breaking his concentration. I glanced at McNally. He was frowning and massaging his forehead.

Suddenly Pleskit stood up from the bench where he was working. *"Krepotzim!"* he cried, letting go a mighty fart as he did. If I didn't know that farts were part of the alien language, I would have been totally offended. As it was, I was still pretty grossed out. McNally just sighed and rolled his eyes.

Pleskit raced across the room and played with some knobs on the wall. The light grew dim and orangey.

"Thinking light," he called over his shoulder, as if answering the question I had in my mind about what he was doing.

He went to a lab table and began taking out equipment — beakers and test tubes that looked a lot like the ones we use here on Earth, plus a lot of other stuff I didn't recognize. Pretty soon he had so much stuff on the table that it looked as if he was running a one-person science fair.

He began singing to himself in what I assume was Hevi-Hevian, punctuating the end of each verse with a burp. Every once in a while he would scurry over to the computer and check the viewscreen. Sometimes he would turn a handle, push a button, or whisper a command. Then he would scurry back to the table.

He had a dozen beakers and bottles working now, filled with mixes and potions of all different colors. Some of them were bubbling. Some were steaming. Some were hissing and popping.

All this time Tim just stood against the wall, his arms crossed over his chest, staring straight ahead, as if nothing was happening.

Pleskit went to a control panel beside the door and

pushed some more buttons. An eerie, low-pitched wail began to quaver through the room.

"Thinking *music*," he explained, without really looking at us.

Back to the lab table. Mixing, stirring, smelling, frowning, tossing stuff out, starting again. More chemicals, more potions. A beaker fell over. Pleskit ignored the bubbling puddle of goo, focusing completely on the steaming purple potion in his hand instead.

"Eegon spritzen plumto dimwakkle!" he cried in disgust, pouring it out.

He hurried back to the wall, pushed some more buttons. "Thinking *smells!*" he cried. Gusts of odor — some delicious, some revolting — began wafting through the room.

He began to zip back and forth between the lab table and the computer. "Yes, yes, yes," he muttered. "No! *Geezbat!*" He turned toward us. "Sorry. Didn't mean to swear."

Then it was as if we didn't exist again as he moved back into his mad-scientist mode. I had never seen such concentration.

Suddenly he began to laugh, a laugh of triumph

and relief. Holding up a clear tube filled with a bubbling purple potion, he cried, "Behold the solution!"

Walking to Tim, he held out the tube.

"Drink this!" he ordered.

Tim took the tube. "Yes, Mast . . . mmmm . . .
mmmm —"

Pleskit sighed. "Don't talk, just *drink!*"

Tim lifted the tube and poured the purple potion
down his throat.

CHAPTER 14

[PLESKIT]
JUDGMENT DAY

I do not think that I have ever worked as hard, thought as hard, as when I made the anti-zombie potion for Tim. When I was finished — or, at least, hoped I was finished, since I still did not know for sure if it was going to work or not — I had him drink it and then stood, watching, with hope and fear raging in my *plinktum.*

After he finished drinking the potion, Tim stood for a moment without moving.

Suddenly he blinked. He flexed his fingers. Then a deep, cleansing belch rose from deep within him.

"Whew," he said. "That's a relief!"

I had my friend back!

Linnsy and McNally began to cheer. My knees trembled, and I felt myself begin to shake. I realized I was on the verge of slipping into *kleptra*. It was only then that I understood how frightened I had been, and how deeply I had been concentrating.

"How do you feel?" I asked.

"Pretty good," said Tim. Notice, he didn't say: "How do you want me to feel?" or "How *should* I feel?" Just: "Pretty good."

I don't think those words have ever sounded so wonderful.

"Sit down!" I said firmly.

"I don't want to," replied Tim.

Never had defiance seemed so sweet!

"I think I need to rest now," I murmured.

"Funny," said Tim. "I feel terrific."

"Come on, you two," said McNally. "I'll have Ralph take you home. Pleskit needs some sack time."

I was barely conscious as I stumbled to my room, barely had energy to summon the air mattress. Flinging myself atop it, I fell quickly into a deep sleep. I had one last thought as I lost consciousness: *Now that I have an antidote, my science fair project is bound to be a winner!*

Zombies of the Science Fair

* * *

When I woke later that evening, I called Tim on the comm device to make sure he was still all right.

"Doin' fine," he said. "Sorry to give you such a scare, Pleskit. That was a pretty stupid thing I did at the science fair today."

"We have a proverb on Hevi-Hevi: Rage makes fools of even the wisest men."

"Whoever said that must have had to live with someone like Jordan," said Tim.

The next day was judging day. I got up early and prepared a large batch of the antidote I had created the night before, which I wanted to add to my display. I also created some new charts and a new computer animation to help explain how it worked.

It turned out that Science Fair Day was a very big deal at school, with lots of parents coming to see all the work the kids had done. A five-person panel of judges—three scientists from the university, a TV weatherman, and the mayor of the city—was going to look at all the projects and choose the ones that would go on to the citywide competition. Also, a team of reporters was allowed into the school for the first time since I had started coming here. As Principal Grand explained it in a call to the Fatherly One: the local news had always covered the science fair, and letting them in was part of getting the school back on a normal footing.

The Fatherly One himself did not come, alas. He had to go to India to visit the prime minister.

Despite Mr. Grand's statement about getting the school back to normal, things were very complicated because of all the security measures they have put in place as a result of my presence. Some of those measures are to protect me from Earthlings who might want to harm me because they are frightened by contact with another species, or simply because—and this really terrified me when I found out about it—they are seeking publicity. Even more embarrassing is the fact that some of the security measures are because we have had problems with other off-worlders trying to sabotage the Fatherly One's mission by getting at me. It is hard to be too critical of Earth's primitive ways when we still have problems of our own.

Anyway, everyone who came into the school had to

go through a very rigorous security check. This was the second large meeting we had had since all the security was put in place. Just like at the PTA Welcome Back night, some people complained bitterly about having to go through the metal detector and the body scanner while others said they thought every school in America ought to have such security devices.

This idea was truly strange and disturbing to me.

While the fair was going, we had to stand beside our projects to explain them and answer questions. I noticed a large crowd of people gathered around Michael's basket and pulley project. People applauded every time he pulled himself into the air.

For security reasons, people were only allowed to approach my booth two at a time. (They did make an exception for the judges.) McNally stuck so close to my side it would have been hard to slip a piece of paper between us. People seemed to find my display either fascinating or offensive. The judges, however, were very impressed — especially the mayor. McNally said that was because any politician would love to have a ray he could use to get people to do whatever he told them.

At the end of the day the results of the judging were announced. Ten of us were to be selected to go to the citywide competition. The judges had chosen one third grader, one fourth grader, two fifth graders, and six of us from sixth grade. Of the sixth grade Ms. Weintraub's class had done the best, with *five* of us being selected: Jordan, Linnsy, Michael, me, and —to everyone's surprise —Tim!

Tim was so excited when his name was called that he let out a big "YESSSSSS!" and began pumping his arm up and down in a strange fashion.

Zombies of the Science Fair

"Jeez," said Jordan. "Are you sure Pleskit didn't use his mind ray to *force* the judges to choose that dweeb?"

Jordan is such a source of negative energy in our class that sometimes I wonder if he is made of antimatter.

I tried to ignore him and concentrate on the sweetness of victory.

My friends and I were going to the city finals!

It was a wonderful moment.

So I'm just as glad I had no inkling of the horror that was awaiting us.

RECOVERED COMMUNICATION (TRANSLATION)

FROM: Skizzdor, waiting and ready on Planet Earth

TO: One who must remain nameless

Glorious Leader:

All is ready for me to make the substitution at the appropriate time.

Our contact tells us we will have a good chance to make the snatch on Friday evening——partly because of the work our on-site agent has done to adjust the schedule to suit our plans.

I know you have been told I was nearly

spotted the other day. Please do not fear. I am confident I escaped detection. The agent who brought you that report was merely trying to curry favor. Rest assured that the Hevi-Hevian brat will be in your hands by Saturday morning. After that . . . well, whatever happens next is up to you.

I know you are looking forward to it!

Let me know if you have any last-minute instructions.

Skizzdor

CHAPTER 15

[T I M]
JUDGE NOT . . .

I couldn't believe I had made the citywide finals for the science fair.

My mother was even more stunboggled than I was.

I did have a slight feeling of guilt because I had done it with the help of Pleskit's Suggestibility Ray. Yet all the ray had done was let me tap my own natural abilities.

I thought about what Linnsy's mom had told us about the kids in our class who take medicine to help them concentrate better. Was this any different? Some people are more able than others to use their brains — and according to what Pleskit and Beezle Whompis had told me, none of us humans is using them at full capacity. Since the ability was part of me, it wasn't unnatural. On the other hand, I hadn't accessed it in a natural way.

I tried to figure out what all that means, but my unenhanced brain wasn't up to the job.

Things at school were pretty good, except for Jordan, who kept making snide remarks about everything Pleskit or I did. I was used to that, of course, but he seemed even worse than usual. I got the feeling he was offended because my project had been deemed as worthy as the one his daddy had bought for him.

The next round of judging was scheduled for Friday night and Saturday morning. The setup was a little different this time. Friday afternoon the finalists from each school were to take their projects to Elbork High and set them up in the gymnasium. Then the kids from each school — there were ten schools in all — had about an hour to come in and explain their projects to the judges.

Our school was scheduled to be the last one presenting on Friday. We ten finalists spent a lot of time debating whether that was a good time slot. I was of the opinion that by being last we would have a good chance to stand out in the judges' minds. Jordan was of the opinion that by Saturday morning they would have forgotten us. He was also of the opinion that any opinion *I* had must be wrong by definition.

The gym at the high school is enormous, big enough to contain two full basketball courts. The custodian had pulled out this kind of folding wall that divided the gym in half, so the high school students could still do gym-type stuff while the science fair finals were going on.

Setup went pretty well, but it was clear there were a lot of good projects from all over the city. By the time Friday night rolled around, I was so tense I could hardly breathe. Mom made me dress up much more than usual and spent a ridiculous amount of time trying to get my hair to look just right. We were barely speaking to each other by the time we left the apartment.

We met Pleskit and McNally at the entrance to the high school. I didn't say anything to Pleskit, but sometimes I wonder how he feels about the fact that his Fatherly One so rarely shows up for this kind of thing. Meenom was a good guy and all, but in some ways it seemed as if Pleskit didn't have much more of a father than I did.

Linnsy and Michael were there already, as was

Zombies of the Science Fair

Calvin Jackson, the third grader who had won. The others came along soon. Jordan was last. He came with his father, who looks sort of like a movie star. I don't know why that should annoy me, but it does.

We went in together. The five judges — a completely different group than had judged at our school — were sitting at a long table. They introduced themselves. Three of them were from the university, one was from a big chemical company that operates here in Syracuse, and one was from a new computer company that had just started up in town.

Our parents and guardians sat in the bleachers behind them, facing us.

Little Calvin was the first to demonstrate his project, which was on lenses. The judges listened to him carefully, nodding and making notes.

I was third. The judges seemed to like what I had done — especially the charts I had made to show the different droplet size and range of the various sprayers. And they all got a chuckle out of Gramma's old-fashioned spray gun.

Linnsy's project actually got some applause, which made the rest of us jealous.

When Jordan did his demonstration, one of the judges leaned forward and said, "You do that all by yourself, young man?"

Jordan blushed, but claimed it was all his own work.

Then it was Pleskit's turn. The judges seemed fascinated by his work and began to ask him all kinds of questions. Finally Pleskit asked if they would like a demonstration.

"I'd like that very much," said Dr. Frobisher, one of the women from the university.

"Tim, would you mind giving me a hand?" asked Pleskit.

I was in the bleachers, sitting with Mom. I glanced at her. She looked surprised, and a little nervous. But she didn't shake her head. So I walked down to where Pleskit was standing.

"Just a small dose, right?" I asked quietly.

He nodded. "Absolutely."

Then he flipped off the safety switch and shot me with the ray.

Once again I felt that peculiar lethargy slip over me — though not nearly as strongly as when I had given myself the superdose the week before.

Pleskit suggested I was feeling very intelligent,

then invited the judges to ask me some math questions. After I answered them with no problem, Dr. Frobisher said, "That appears very impressive, Pleskit. On the other hand, since we don't know what Tim's ability was before you dosed him with the Suggestibility Ray, it's hard to say how effective it really was. How do we know he's not just a natural math whiz?"

This idea caused Jordan to laugh out loud.

"I believe that human sensory ability is also considerably more acute than most people realize," said Pleskit. "Would a demonstration of that be of interest?"

"Absolutely," said Dr. Thornton, the guy from the chemical company.

Pleskit turned to me. "Tim, I believe your nose is far more powerful than you ever knew. In fact, I'm sure of it. Why not try it out and see?"

I took a deep breath. Suddenly the air was rich with scents and smells, such a blizzard of them that I felt overwhelmed at first. I wondered if this was what the world smells like to a dog.

Then I noticed that something was wrong — really wrong.

I sniffed again . . . and again.

Bruce Coville

Each person in the room had a distinct odor. With my nose as powerful as it was right then, I could have picked out any one of them in a crowd of thousands.

But despite these distinct differences, every one of them had a basic odor that was unmistakably *human*.

All but two. Pleskit, of course, did not smell human.

Neither did the judge at the end of the table, the one from the new computer company.

CHAPTER 16

[PLESKIT]
ATTACK OF THE ZOMBIES

"What do you smell?" I asked.

To my astonishment, Tim replied, "I smell an alien."

Then he pointed to the judge at the end of the table.

A dead silence fell over the gymnasium. After a second the judge that Tim had pointed to began to laugh.

"Well, I guess your little invention isn't quite all it's cracked up to be, is it, Pleskit?"

I didn't know what to say. I didn't believe Tim was wrong. On the other hand, if he was right, it meant something really bad was going on. I didn't want to press the situation, for fear of pushing the fake judge into some desperate action.

Bruce Coville

As it turned out, it didn't make any difference what I said. "Grab him, McNally!" cried Tim's mother. "Get the alien creep!"

McNally started forward—not toward the judge, but toward me. I assume he was going to put himself between the judge and me, just in case Tim was right. But the "judge" was a lot closer. He vaulted over the table and snatched the Suggestibility Ray out of my hand.

Then he turned it on McNally full force.

"Stop right where you are!" he ordered.

McNally stopped, stood absolutely still, not even blinking.

A confusion of shouting broke out in the bleachers. People were getting up to run—some toward the renegade judge, some toward the exits. The other judges had leaped to their feet as well.

The renegade turned the Suggestibility Ray on them, swinging it back and forth. "Don't move!" he ordered. "Don't move, don't move, don't move."

The judges stopped in their tracks.

The renegade sprang forward and snatched one of the lenses from little Calvin's display. Stretching out one arm, he was able to hold it in front of the ray gun.

Zombies of the Science Fair

Then he switched on the ray again. The purple light was diffused by the lens so that it covered a much wider area. Scanning the ray back and forth he kept repeating, "You want to hold still, you want to hold still, you *want* to hold still!"

You could see that at first people struggled against his command. But the initial dose of the ray was enough to slow them down—which bought him time to give everyone in the crowd a shot of it.

The second dose slowed them down even more.

By the third pass, people were barely twitching.

He swung the ray on Tim and me, as well. I wasn't sure how it would affect Tim, since I had already given him a slight dose of the ray. I was pretty sure how it would affect me—which is to say, not at all. I had designed the ray for the human brain, not the brain of someone from Hevi-Hevi.

My suspicion was right. When the so-called judge looked at me and said, "You want to stand still," I didn't feel the slightest urge to do so.

But I did anyway. I figured there was no reason for *him* to know the ray hadn't affected me.

At least, not yet.

He looked around the room and laughed. Then he took a small communications device from his pocket. Flipping it open, he began speaking in Galactic Standard.

"Urkding? Skizzdor here. Things just got a little . . . complicated." A pause while he listened, then: "No . . . no, I have everything under control. It's just that there was an unexpected development, and we should make the pickup as soon as possible." Another pause to listen, then words that sent a cold chill into my *clinkus.* "I know that's earlier than planned. Just do it! I'll have the ambassador's brat waiting at the side door for you!"

Muttering angrily to himself, Skizzdor shut the comm device. Then he snapped his head up at the sound of one of the gym doors opening.

It can't be Urkding already! I thought desperately.

I was right. It was one of the school custodians, stepping through the door in the divider wall.

Skizzdor snatched up the Suggestibility Ray and ran toward the custodian. As soon as his back was turned, I grabbed something else —the antidote. I ordered Tim to open his mouth. To my relief he was still responding to my suggestions. I poured a few drops onto his tongue. He blinked, then shivered.

Zombies of the Science Fair

"Man, Pleskit, we're in big trouble!" he whispered.

From behind us, I heard Skizzdor ordering the custodian to hold still.

"Come on," I said. "Let's get out of here."

"I can't leave my mother," said Tim.

"He's not after your mother! He wants me. I just want you to come with me because I figure we'll have a better chance of stopping him if we work together. Come on, let's go."

We took off for the door at the far side of the gym.

Behind us we heard Skizzdor shout with anger, "Stop! Stop, you two!"

We didn't stop, of course. Why should we? We weren't under his control.

But the rest of the people in the gym were.

"Stop them!" he bellowed. "Stop those boys."

As one, the people in the gym — our friends, our friends' parents, McNally, the other judges, even Tim's mom — began shambling toward us.

CHAPTER 17

[TIM]
"GET THEM!"

I had already learned that my brain was capable of far more than I'd realized.

When the zombies started chasing us, I realized this was true of my body, too. I covered the distance to that door in record time. Unfortunately, it was locked.

Pleskit and I looked at each other in horror. The zombies were shambling toward us, their arms raised, their eyes wide. It looked like a scene from *Night of the Living Dead.* The worst thing was seeing my mom as one of them.

We had one thing on our side. The zombies were moving in a slow, deliberate fashion. I guess when you drain someone's willpower, you can force them to do something, but you can't make them do it well.

That didn't stop Skizzdor from shouting, "Faster! Faster, you fools!"

"Faster!" mumbled the zombies. "Faster!"

But they didn't go faster. They just kept coming at us in the same slow, deliberate fashion. It was a little like being menaced by a steamroller.

The zombies were in the middle of the gym. The next closest door was in the divider wall —which was on the other side of them. But Pleskit and I were so much faster than they were that I thought maybe if we ran around the edge of the gym, we could beat them to the door.

Maybe.

Quickly I told Pleskit what I had in mind. "Let's go for it!" he gasped.

We took off running.

"Get them!" shrieked Skizzdor.

"Get them, get them, get them," droned the zombies, swinging around as a group to move after us. They shambled toward the wall of the gym. Pleskit and I literally ran for our lives. Jordan, his eyes glazed and his face blank, was at the head of the pack. McNally and my mother were close behind him. As we passed the midpoint of the gym, the zombie pack turned again to follow us. But we had crossed the danger point.

We got to the door and yanked it open.

The lights in this section of the gym were out. We stumbled into the darkness.

The zombies reached the door behind us. The narrow opening slowed them down because they were all trying to push their way through it at the same time.

"Ouch!" I cried as I bumped into something. In the dim light that filtered past the zombie-jammed doorway, I figured out that it was a vaulting box.

"Come on!" urged Pleskit.

"Get them!" chanted the zombies.

I got past the vaulting box but wasn't able to run as fast as I wanted for fear I would bump into something else. It wasn't the pain I was afraid of—it was the chance that if I ran too fast I would knock myself unconscious, in which case the zombies would get me.

When we got to the far side of the darkened gym we made our way along a wall until we found a doorway. It swung open. I groped for a light switch. When I found it, the glare of light temporarily dazzled us.

Blinking, squinting, I realized we had stumbled into the girls' locker room.

Normally I would have been horrified, curious, and embarrassed. Now I was just horrified — not because of where we were, but because I could hear the zombies shambling through the darkness after us. I slammed the door shut and cursed the fact that I couldn't lock it without a key.

I looked around, desperately seeking a place to hide. Then I had a brainstorm. "Up there!" I cried to Pleskit.

"The ceiling?" he asked, puzzled.

"I think those tiles will lift up," I said. "Come on, give me a boost so I can see."

We scrambled onto one of the benches that went between the rows of lockers, then Pleskit hoisted me up so I could climb on top of the lockers. The ceiling was about four feet above them. I pushed against one of the tiles. Bingo! It rose up, revealing an open space about two feet high above it.

We could hear the zombies scrabbling at the door. It wouldn't be long before they had it open.

"Come on," I said, reaching a hand down.

Soon Pleskit was beside me. I boosted him up into

the space. "Be careful," I whispered as he climbed in. "Those tiles won't hold our weight. Make sure you stay on the metal crossbars."

Even those were iffy, and I winced as I saw one of them bend. Even so, I climbed up beside him. We moved the tile back into place, leaving just a crack so we could peer down.

Seconds later the zombies got the door open.

"Get them! Get them!" they chanted as they stumbled into the room. They marched slowly forward, looking from side to side. They went directly underneath us without realizing where we were. As they neared the far end of the locker room, they began to slow down, clearly confused. As I looked down at them, something bothered me. Before I could figure out what it was, I was distracted by Pleskit whispering, "If only we could give them the antidote."

It was a great idea. Except how do you get two dozen or so zombies to take an antidote — especially if they are mindlessly bent on "getting" you?

Suddenly I had an answer!

Unfortunately, before I could explain it to Pleskit, Skizzdor burst into the locker room.

"Where are they?" he shrieked.

The zombies, having no idea where we were, remained silent.

Unfortunately, while the zombies were mindless, Skizzdor was not. "You have superb noses!" he said. "You can smell with incredible precision. NOW FIND THOSE KIDS!"

The zombies began to sniff. From personal experience, I was pretty sure it wouldn't take long for them to figure out where we were.

"Come on," I whispered to Pleskit. "We've got to get out of here."

"But where?" he asked.

"Back to the science fair."

"What?"

"No time to explain. Come on, let's move!"

I moved more than I intended. Trying to lift one of the tiles so we could climb down, I crashed through another one and landed on top of one of the lockers.

"Get them!" shrieked Skizzdor.

CHAPTER 18

[PLESKIT]
AIR PATROL

When Tim suggested we go back to the gym,
I thought he had lost his mind.

When he fell through the ceiling, I was sure of it.

But by then, we had no choice. The zombies knew
where we were, and were after us. I jumped down
beside him, then helped him scramble from the locker
top down to the bench.

Skizzdor, much faster than the zombies, was trying to
get through them to reach us. But they completely jammed
the narrow area between the lockers, so though he was
shrieking in frustration for them to get out of the way, we
had time to get out of the locker room ahead of him.

Bruce Coville

The gym wasn't quite so dark now, since it was getting light spill from both doors — the one to the locker room, and the one that led back to the science fair. Now I could see the forms of all the equipment, though I didn't know what it was called.

At the opposite end of the gym, barely visible, was another door. It had been propped open — probably by the custodian who had come through with the broom.

"That way!" said Tim, pointing to the door.

"I thought you said you wanted to go back to the science fair!"

"Yeah, but I want to take the long way, so we can get a bigger lead on them."

The moment of delay was nearly fatal. We heard the zombies coming through the door behind us. No time to argue the point, and Tim had an idea — whatever it was — which was more than I could say at the moment.

So we went in his direction.

I tripped over a floor mat. *"Zgribnick!"* I cried.

Despite the approaching zombies, Tim stopped to help me up. We stumbled forward again, but the lost time hurt us — as did a new problem.

Zombies of the Science Fair

"I knew there was something wrong in the locker room!" cried Tim.

I saw at once what he meant. Skizzdor had not sent all the zombies in to get us. He had left another batch of them waiting in the gym, and now they were blocking our path.

Zombies ahead of us, zombies behind us.

"That way!" cried Tim, pointing to our left. He began running toward the bleachers that extended out from the wall.

I followed his lead, though I couldn't figure what good it would do us.

We scrambled up the bleachers.

The zombies shambled toward us, slowly but inexorably.

"This way," said Tim. "I've got another idea!"

I followed him along the top row of seats — and suddenly I thought I knew what his idea was. Ahead of us, tied to the wall, were a pair of thick ropes. "Climbing ropes," explained Tim as he began to fumble at the knot holding one in place.

I started to work at the other.

The zombies began to cluster below us. Their slow,

awkward movements made it hard for them to climb the bleachers. The ones at the rear pressed forward. The ones at the front began to trip their way up the steps. We waited . . . waited . . . waited. The zombies were crawling up the steps, getting close, closer, too close, way too close . . .

"Now!" cried Tim.

Pushing out from the wall, we swung over their heads, far out into the gym. At the far end of the arc I let go of my rope — and landed on something incredibly springy.

"Pleskit!" cried Tim as I bounced into the air. "Get off the trampoline and follow me!"

"I'm trying!" I cried as I bounced again. "I'm trying!"

Fortunately, the zombies were tangled up in themselves as they tried to get off the bleachers and turn back in our direction.

"Get them!" shrieked Skizzdor. "Get them!"

He wasn't standing that far from the trampoline. I had had plenty of practice bouncing on my bed. Circumstances were desperate. I decided to take a chance. Instead of trying to decrease my bounces, I made them bigger. *Boing. Boing!*

Zombies of the Science Fair

Boing!!

I flew off the trampoline and landed directly on Skizzdor, who collapsed beneath me.

"Nice shot!" cried Tim.

Skizzdor moaned but seemed to be unconscious.

I staggered to my feet and moaned myself as I realized the zombies were still after us.

"Come on!" cried Tim. "Let's get out of here!"

We bolted for the far door, pulled it shut behind us. It wouldn't stop the zombies, but it would slow them down.

We pelted down the hallway, back through the other gym door, knowing that the zombies would follow our trail, rather than doing the smart thing and coming back by the short way.

"Okay, what's your idea?" I panted.

Tim told me.

"Let's do it!" I cried.

We hurried to his display and grabbed his grand- mother's spray gun. "What's in there now?" I asked as we hurried to my display.

"Nothing but water," he said.

"Good, we probably need to dilute this anyway." While Tim unscrewed the cap at the end of the spray gun, I opened the antidote. I poured it into the spray gun. "Shake it up," I said.

We could hear the zombies coming down the hall.

Still following Tim's plan, we scurried over to Michael's pulley display and scrambled into the bucket.

The zombies were almost at the door.

"I sure hope this will hold both of us," said Tim.

"I hope he designed the pulley ratio so that I can lift us!" I responded as I began to pull on the ropes.

Creaking and complaining, the pulleys did their job, multiplying my effort into a much greater force. Slowly we began to rise from the gymnasium floor. When we were as high as we wanted, I wound the rope around my hand another time.

"I'm not sure how long I can hold this," I whispered.

"Just another few minutes," whispered Tim encouragingly. "You can do it! I know you can!"

The zombies were at the door. We ducked our heads so that we were just peering over the edge of the bucket.

Once they were in the room the zombies stopped in confusion. They looked around, then sniffed the air again. A moment later they were shambling in our direction.

Zombies of the Science Fair

Soon they had gathered in a knot below us.

"All right, lower the bucket!" whispered Tim.

I let us down a few feet so we were dangling over their heads but still out of reach.

Groaning mindlessly, the zombies stretched their arms toward us.

Tim leaned out of the bucket and began to pump the spray gun.

CHAPTER 19

[TIM]
SKIZZDOR

As soon as the purple mist of the antidote drifted over the zombies, I could see them begin to relax. Their mindless groans stopped. They dropped their arms to their sides. They twitched a few times, then blinked, then shook their heads.

A moment later a babble of voices broke out. The words were angry, confused, frightened, but—and this was the beautiful thing—each person was shouting something different.

My favorite was my mother, who shouted, "Timothy, you get down from there!"

Leaning over the edge of the bucket, which made

it tip dangerously, I said, "Wait just a minute, Mom. The rat that did this to you is still on the loose — and still dangerous. Pleskit knocked him out, but I suspect he'll be back in a minute."

The crowd began to mutter, some angrily, some in fear. It was wonderful to hear the difference in their voices.

"Listen!" I cried, holding up my hands. "I'm afraid he's got a weapon of some kind. If he realizes you're free of his power, he might use it. But if you'll all pretend you're still zombies, I think we can catch him."

Dr. Frobisher and McNally quickly got the idea, and convinced the others to go along with it. So they were all standing below us, stretching their arms up and groaning mindlessly when Skizzdor came limping back into the gym.

"Good!" he cried. "You've trapped them."

He hobbled over to where Pleskit and I were dangling in the air. "Get back," he ordered the people, assuming that they were still zombies. "Get back."

Muttering and shuffling, the crowd backed away, forming a circle around him.

He looked up at us. "You boys might as well come down," he said triumphantly. "You can't escape now!"

Which was when McNally conked him on the head.

CHAPTER 20

[PLESKIT]
A LETTER HOME

FROM: Pleskit Meenom, on the always interesting Planet Earth
TO: Maktel Geebrit, on the much-missed Planet Hevi-Hevi

Dear Maktel:

Well, there it is——the story of how I survived my latest *glikksa* idea. Believe me, I will never again mess around with an Earthling's mind. It leads to more trouble than it is worth.

I have only a few details left to tell. After Tim and I had lowered ourselves to the floor,

I helped McNally find the way to peel off Skizzdor's mask. You should have heard the gasps from the Earthlings when they saw his pebbly orange face.

McNally called in reinforcements, hoping to catch Skizzdor's cohort, Urkding. But Urkding never showed up—probably because he had some way of knowing their plan had fallen apart.

It will probably not surprise you to learn that Skizzdor was working for our old enemy Harr-giss. So even though Harr-giss himself remains in custody, his agents are still trying to sabotage our efforts here on Earth.

"I don't know why he doesn't just sit back and let you do the job for him," snapped the Fatherly One, in the first flush of his anger.

He was most upset with me for creating the Suggestibility Ray.

However, his anger was softened by two things:

First, I think he is starting to feel a great deal of guilt over the amount of time he spends away from the embassy.

Second, if it had not been for the Suggestibility Ray, Skizzdor might have succeeded in his scheme to kidnap me.

"Even so," said the Fatherly One, "you must not tamper with the Earthlings' brains like this."

"But think how beneficial this technology would be for them!" I cried.

"And have you forgotten the laws forbidding us to interfere with the development of a species?" he replied sharply. "This could cause us no end of trouble with the Trading Federation."

I sighed. "Must we erase the Earthlings' memory of what has happened?"

The Fatherly One looked at me in shock. "What an immoral idea! It would be totally unethical to take from a being the memory of an experience it has already had. Really, Pleskit, I have been neglecting your education. I must spend more time with you."

So things didn't work out all bad after all, since I have been most anxious for the Fatherly One to do exactly that.

The Fatherly One has hinted that it might actually work out for you to come to visit. I hope, hope, hope that this is true. It would be great for you to meet my new friends and get a firsthand look at this planet. Strange as it might seem, I am actually starting to like the place!

Please write soon.

Fremmix Bleeblom!

Your pal,

Pleskit

SPECIAL BONUS:

On the following pages you will find Part Five of *Disaster on Geembol Seven*—Pleskit's story of what happened on the last planet where he lived before coming to Earth.

This story is being told in six installments, one at the end of each of the first six books of the Sixth-Grade Alien series.

The final thrilling chapter will appear in Book Six: *Class Pet Catastrophe*!

DISASTER ON GEEMBOL SEVEN

PART FIVE:
"AN ANCIENT WRONG"

FROM: Pleskit Meenom, on Planet Earth
TO: Maktel Geebrit, on Planet Hevi-Hevi
Dear Maktel:

As I have been promising, here is more about what happened to me on Geembol Seven.

Just to remind you: The Fatherly One and I had been on the planet only a few days when he took me out to the Moondance Celebration. During the festivities I spotted a six-eyed boy named Derrvan who seemed to be in great distress. I followed him to the waterfront, where I was yanked into a hidden elevator and taken deep beneath the surface of the planet.

The being who had pulled me in was one of those illegal combinations of biological and mechanical parts you and I have been taught to fear since we were little: a construct. It turned out that Derrvan's father had worked with the constructs. But before Derrvan and Balteeri could tell me what they wanted we were pursued deeper into the planet, to an underground city *filled* with constructs. Balteeri led us to a chapel where he asked the *serha* in charge, a female construct named Dombalt, to tell me their story.

Serha Dombalt stared at me from the shadow of her hooded cloak. "How much do you know about the history of the constructs?"

"Only what everyone knows," I replied. Then I felt the coldness of *pizumpta*. What everyone "knows" about the constructs, of course, is that they were the evil invention of a warped genius, that they were the implacable enemies of biological beings, that they would just as soon kill you as look at you, that . . . well, I knew a whole lot of things that weren't very nice and that should have left me terrified. Yet none of what I "knew" seemed to match the experience I had had so far with *these* constructs.

Of course, the other thing everyone knows is that despite occasional scare stories about "construct sightings," the creatures had been wiped out in the Delfiner War.

"We have a saying," murmured *Serha* Dombalt, interrupting my thoughts. "No matter how much you know, there's always more to the story."

"Especially when so much of what you think you know is wrong," growled Balteeri.

Serha Dombalt raised a hand to silence him. "The saying is valid no matter how much you know," she said quietly. "Even if it's all true." She turned back to me. "This much of what I suspect you have been told *is* true: The first constructs were made over a thousand

grinnugs ago, long before the birth of the Trading Federation. It was a time of turmoil in the galaxy, for a great——and unnecessary—— struggle between religion and science was shaking systems to their roots.

"Three things happened that led to the Delfiner War. The first was the perfection of the technology that let doctors replace any lost limb or organ with a mechanical sub- stitute. This was actually accomplished by Derrvan's grandfather."

I started to ask how Derrvan's grandfather could have been involved in something that happened so long ago, but quickly realized there were a dozen ways it was possible, anything from the time-warping effects of sub-light-speed travel to a long term in sus- pended animation, to . . . well, a variety of things I had probably never even heard of.

"The second major step toward the war," continued *Serha* Dombalt, "came when those replacement body parts were refined so that they exceeded the original biology, making many constructs stronger or more adept than 'organics,' as nonconstruct beings began to refer to themselves." She sighed. "This created an undercurrent of jealousy that was ripe for fanning into the flames of hate.

"The third step came with the perfection of yet another technology, one that allowed a body to regrow any lost part. When this happened, a number of fanatical religious groups began claiming that only a natural body was acceptable in the eyes of whatever god they worshiped, and that constructs were 'abominations' or 'works of the Great Evil' or 'Children of *Refuljus*' or . . . well, any of a thousand other things.

"In this way the constructs became the focal point for a clash between science and religion that had been brewing for hundreds of *grinnugs*. Remember, this was early in the history of the Connected Galaxy, and the Great Understanding had not yet even been dreamed of.

"The war started small but spread fast,

as often happens with these things. But this was not merely a war between constructs and organics, or between two planets. It was between science and religion, and its flames swept the galaxy in a wave of destruction unlike anything seen before or—thank all that is good—since.

"Each side, of course, believed it was totally in the right. Fortunately, there were beings of goodwill on both sides, who soon recoiled in horror from the destruction that had been unleashed, and began to seek for a peace. Though the war was about far more than the constructs, we had become a symbol of the clash, and we were the final sticking point in the solution.

"Eventually a secret agreement was reached, largely through the efforts of Derrvan's father."

I glanced at the six-eyed boy. I think it was the first time I had seen him smile.

"That agreement called for the Geembolians to accept the remaining constructs—

and there were not that many of us, for an enormous number had died during the war—here on their planet. Or, to be more precise, *in* their planet. In return, the Geembolians insisted that the deal remain a secret, for we were still considered both a shame and a danger."

Serha Dombalt's voice became sharp with anger.

"Did money change hands? Almost certainly. Did the common people of Geembol know about the deal? Possible, but highly unlikely. We have remained here ever since, the secret shame of the Geembolian government, sealed in our underground world, where we were allowed to live, but just barely. We are illegal in the greater galaxy, through old laws that remained long after the war was over. But most people think we are gone, and use us simply as a story to frighten young ones into behaving. Here on Geembol there is an elite corps of construct hunters, a secret service that devotes all its energy to keeping us from escaping."

"But if this happened so long ago, why are there so many of you now?" I asked, feeling confused.

"Pride," said Balteeri. "We refuse to accept the judgment of others, and so we live, and we marry, and we reproduce, and all our children are constructs, too. We replace limbs and organs not because they are defective, but because there are better things available."

I felt a tightening in my *clinkus*. I would hate to be the child of a construct.

Serha Dombalt sighed.

"The Delfiner War is still taught in school, of course, as it should be, since it was the last of the galaxy-wide conflicts. But, like the history of most wars, it is taught badly, and the 'facts' depend on which side is telling the story. Little thought or question is given to the constructs and what happened to them. We have lived beyond the notice of most of the rest of the galaxy for these many hundred *grinnugs*. However, now we are in grave danger."

I looked at her curiously. "Why now, after all this time?"

She placed her hand against the stone wall. "This underground city that has sheltered us for so long is about to collapse. That collapse might not happen for another Geembolian year. It might as easily happen tomorrow. The timing is not certain, but the fact that it *will* happen is as certain as stone."

I glanced around nervously. "What do you mean?"

"The planet is shifting," explained the *serha*, "as all living planets do. Tectonic pressure is building, pressure that must soon be released in a grinding earthquake—an earthquake that will destroy the city, send it crashing down around us. When that happens we will be buried alive, and the place that was once our shelter will become our tomb. We *have* to leave here. But the Geembolians have us bottled in, and turn a deaf ear to our pleas."

"They don't believe you?" I asked in horror.

Zombies of the Science Fair

"They don't even listen," said *Serha* Dombalt. "We are a bad memory, a blot on their conscience, a mistake no one wants to remember, a secret kept from their own people. The ancient bargain still rankles, and the planetary government will not admit that we are even here, much less that we are in danger. The death of our city will close a chapter of their history they would rather forget anyway."

"They'd rather let you die than admit they were wrong?" I asked in astonishment.

"Such are the ways of power," said *Serha* Dombalt. Her voice was remarkably calm, given what she had just told me.

"I still don't understand what this has to do with me," I said, feeling more nervous than ever.

Balteeri spoke up. "I originally went to seek Derrvan, who is our last link to the outside world. I went alone, and barely escaped the construct hunters. But when I returned to Geembol with Derrvan, I learned of your Fatherly One's trade mission. He has credibility here. He will be a source of money for the planet. We want you to get him to speak to the Geembolian leaders on our behalf."

I felt myself quivering on the edge of *kleptra*. The Fatherly One has long taught me that the messenger who brings bad news is never welcome, and is usually blamed for the news itself, even if he or she has nothing to do with it. He has also told me that the Geembolians are very sensitive about their image. For him to take such an action would destroy his mission, and strike a terrible blow at the life he is trying to build for us. This was his first major outpost. How could I ask such a thing of him?

As if to show how petty my concerns really were, a sudden rumbling shook the walls of the building where we sat. I shouted in terror and my *sphen-gnut-ksher* emitted a burst of sparks.

From outside the chapel I could hear shouts, and a distant scream of pain.

"Is this it?" I cried, fighting desperately

to keep myself from slipping into *kleptra*. "Is this——"

My words were cut off by Balteeri grabbing me. He dragged me under a stone table. I could see *Serha* Dombalt and Derrvan sheltering under another table on the far side of the room. Stones fell from the ceiling, one landing but inches from where I had sat while listening to the *serha*'s story.

I don't know how long the rumbling and shaking continued. I think it was a very short time. It felt like several *grinnugs*. Even when it stopped I did not feel safe.

"Is the city collapsing *now*?" I asked, fighting to control the quaver in my voice.

Serha Dombalt crawled out from under her table. "This is not the end," she said, as she reached down to help Derrvan to his feet. "It is merely what we live with these days——a small warning of the cataclysm to come."

I tried to imagine experiencing such terror on a daily basis. But though the Fatherly One claims my imagination is out of control,

I could not think what such a thing must be like.

"All right," I whispered, knowing I was stepping into trouble I could not begin to understand. "I'll help you."

To be continued . . .

A GLOSSARY OF ALIEN TERMS

Following are definitions for the alien words and phrases that appear for the first time in this book. Definitions of alien words used in earlier Sixth-Grade Alien books can be found in the volume where they were first used.

The number after a definition indicates the chapter where the term first appears.

For most words we are only giving the spelling. In actual usage many would, of course, be accompanied by smells and/or body sounds.

DIMWAKKLE: Turn, change, transform. (13)

EEGON: A word used for addressing unanswerable questions to the universe. Though it means "why," it is invariably used in the context of "why *me*?" (13)

GEEZBAT: Hevi-Hevian curse word; not suitable for translating in a children's book. (13)

GEEZBORKIM: To move one's hind end. (3)

GIBBLESPRATTEN: An expression of disgust. Over several centuries this word has been condensed from the much longer phrase *"Fangula eegon gibble tumputt spratten pumtutti"* (literally, "Why must the world always bite me on the butt?"). This was the central life question of the philosophers known as the Northern Depressives. Though the movement has been discredited, the phrase, and the question it implies, linger on. (10)

GLIKKSA: Ill-advised or, more vulgarly, idiotic; the word derives from an early ruler of the Hevi-Hevian empire popularly remembered as Glikksa the Fool (sometimes "Glikksa the Bonehead"), widely considered the worst ruler in the planet's history, primarily because of his decision to build a city over what turned out to be a vast subterranean wampfield. (For more details see article "Sunken City of Luksanntia," in volume 24,982 of the *Encyclopedia Galactica*.) (20)

GRINNUG: A galactic measure of time, roughly equivalent to 427 Earth days. The unit, which was created by averaging the length of the years of the initial ten member planets of the Trading Federation, is considered annoying and out of date. Unfortunately, it is so entrenched in popular usage that no one has been able to come up with a suitable replacement for it. (serial episode)

KREPOT: Quick, rapid, fast. (3)

KREPOTZIM!: Literally: "In a flash!" (The exclamation point is always present.) This word is a favorite of stage magicians on Hevi-Hevi, who are fond of creating great flashes of light and sound as they work their illusions. The word is an ancient one, and most scholars trace it to Ellio Barcadium, the great poet magician of the First Empire. (7)

PLUMTO: *Plonkus* droppings, a particularly vile-smelling animal waste product. (See glossary of Book 2 for a description of the *plonkus*.) (13)

SPRITZEN: Touch, turn one's hand to. (13)

YERTZTIKKIA: A kind of stew made from *klug* root and *skakka* meat, usually seasoned with crushed water-bugs. Originally developed by workers in the northern wampfields, the dish was taken up by the famous chef Snorzel Ch-Forkis and became something of a fad among the rich for a few years. (3)

Note: It is not always easy to make a direct translation from Hevi-Hevian to the language of Earth, partly because of the many subtleties expressed by smell and body sounds, partly because their grammar is quite different from ours. However, by using the words above we can see that the phrase *"Eegon spritzen plumto dimwakkle?"* becomes, roughly, "Why must everything I touch turn to *plonkus* droppings?"—a cry of despair first made popular by young artists during Hevi-Hevi's infamous "Dreary Period."